*A Beautiful Nightmare Story*

L.C. SON

# Dedication

~ To my husband, my living gift. Every day with you is like Christmas. ~

**One Winter's Kiss**
**A Beautiful Nightmare Story**

**Copyright © 2021 by L.C. Son**

All rights reserved. No part of this publication may be reproduced, distributed, or transmitted in any form or by any means, including photocopying, recording, or other electronic or mechanical methods, without the prior written permission of the publisher, except in the case of brief quotations embodied in critical reviews and certain other noncommercial uses permitted by copyright law.
This book and all parts of the Beautiful Nightmare Universe and its collection is a work of fiction. Names, characters, businesses, places, events, and incidents are either the products of the author's imagination or used in a fictional manner. Any resemblance to actual persons, living or dead is purely coincidental.

**www.LCSonBooks.com**

## Prologue

"*How shall I kiss you,*" Lux whispers as the corner of his lips graze my earlobe. My heart thumps at his gracious inquiry. Tiny goosebumps erupt all over my arms and I wonder if he can feel my skin prickling beneath his warm and sturdy grip.

"Answer me, sweetness," Lux demands while his fingers trail down the length of my forearm as his right arm tightens around my waist, bringing me closer to him.

"Everywhere," I breathe, panting with desperation. Tightening my already closed eyes, I dare not open them for fear once I see the glow of his sun-spun eyes deepen into my own, I'll be completely lost to his lure.

I've waited for what feels like an eternity to be in this position. In his embrace. Long days and nights have I pondered what it would be like to be lost in abandon and in the hold of Luxor Decanter. Not once did I think my fantasy would equate to reality. How could such a stately and supernatural being such as he even care for a mere mortal as me.

But, alas, here we are.

"As you wish," he croons in response, his tone melodic. From the first touch of his lips upon my skin as his tongue laps the ravine of my neck to the moment he crushes his mouth to mine, I am lost. I know not the woman I've become in his presence. I am overcome with a giddy, girl-like manner but I can't help it.

He does this to me.

Even more, I want him.

And I want him to kiss me everywhere.

Yes, *everywhere*.

Although his hold on me is strong, Lux's kiss is sweet, gentle, yet intentional. As our tongues intertwine as one, every moment we've ever shared replays like an everlasting love song in my mind. From our first hello a year ago, our instant connection, our first dance at the ball, and now at this very minute, a lovesick fever pulsates within me I never knew was capable.

Pushing me between the corners of the closet door and an adjacent walnut curio, I feel both the thump of his heartbeat and his manhood raging beneath the fabric of his clothes. Pulling away from the lock and tether of our lips, he stares at me, granting me a shy yet knowing glance before once more thrusting his tongue in my mouth, as he controls our passionate posture.

"Everywhere, eh?" Lux smiles, his golden eyes beaming with hopefulness as his thumb strums the zipper of my dress until I am clothed in nothing but my bra and panties.

"Yes," I sigh, leaning my head back to see the glittery specks of snow circling in the tiny glass globes on my dresser. A small smile curves the corners of my mouth as I recall the day Lux gave me the tiny ice rink snow globe once I learned how to ice skate.

I don't have time to linger in the memory as Lux lifts me from the corner, wrapping my legs around his waist, holding me just shy above the protrusion I feel beneath his belt buckle, and walks us to the bed. Nestling his head on my black laced bra, he plants two soft kisses at the helm of my cleavage as he takes a deep breath, inhaling my scent wholly.

"Mmm...Winter, you smell so good. You're my own pretty little sugar plum, aren't you?" Lux softly says as he lays me down into the bouquet of pillows on the bed.

"Yes, all yours," I reply, running my hand through his cascading, deep brown hair that hangs just above his cheekbone. He smiles as I do and a low growl bellows through him and I know it's taking everything within him to keep his wolf at bay.

"But that's not all you are. Is it, Winter?" Lux growls his words into my mouth with a kiss and his hold on me strengthens, as he grips my arms above my head, keeping me under his complete surrender. His teeth grapple my bra and his canines tear through the lace and his face beams at my newfound bareness before him.

A wickedly sexy grin crosses his face as he glares at me and I can do nothing but babble incoherently as my passion builds within me, but his hold on me stays steadfast.

"What, baby? Cat got your tongue?" Lux teases as he licks around my belly button to the sides of my thighs. A moan is all I have to give in reply, and he groans a grizzly chuckle as he continues lapping the insides of my thighs, moving his head just above the laced hem of my panties.

"I'm still waiting, sweetness," he demands once more, gripping the lace between his teeth. Pushing

*Prologue*

my pelvis up to his chin, my moans become more desperate. I've waited for what seems like forever for this moment, but this is complete torture. All I want is to feel the pleasure he brings. Whatever inquiry he has is lost on me. All I want is him.

"Answer me, Winter!" Lux pleas, releasing the hem from his mouth and the elasticity stings as it hits my belly, bringing me back to the moment. His lustful eyes search mine with needful desire as he looks up at me, hovering just above my sweet spot. Everything in me wishes he'd tear into the last remaining garment on my body as he did my bra, but it's clear he's not budging until I answer his question.

"What else are you, sweetness? *Who are you?*" he says while taking in another deep breath between my thighs. "*Ahh—you smell so sweet, Winter,*" Lux whispers as if he's talking directly to my body as he rests his head on my knee, pushing my legs further apart. "I just need you to say it, baby. Tell me who you are." His plea is desperate and his shoulders hunch in exhaustion as he awaits my reply.

As much as I wish for us to finally unite as one, I know he will not continue without the words he longs to hear. Necessary words that break the barriers of what once was. Words that bond our hearts, souls, and bodies forever.

"I am yours. Your wife," I answer quietly, lightly dragging my fingers through his hair.

Once more, Lux looks up at me from between my legs. This time I see more than the wolf I first met on that cold winter's morning behind his eyes. *I see my husband.*

My one true love.

But this moment almost didn't happen.

# ONE YEAR AGO…

# Chapter One

## *Winter*

Staring out my bedroom window, I watch as the last autumn leaf falls to the ground. It is now evident. Winter is here. Not bound to the general measure of the solstice, winters in Nova Scotia peak early. Soon, the ground will be blanketed in thick, white snow. The whales have long since retreated to warmer shores and our once bustling island will be limited to offshore fishers, merchant ships, and those who call this place home.

But more will come.

It is for this reason I know this winter season will be different from all others.

They are coming. The supernaturals. Vampires. Wolves. *Others*.

While I was only a child when they last arrived over a decade ago, I still remember it like it was yesterday. I've been counting the days, months, and even years to this very day.

Recalling the pageantry of their last visit to the manor I call my home still pulsates my heart with a deep longing that I've yet to comprehend. I suppose my expectations are akin to a child awaiting Christmas morning, but I dare say today couldn't have come soon enough for me.

The Altrinion-Vampires and wolves were all elegant, beautiful, and mysteriously marvelous to behold. Nothing like the Scourge Vampires most humans are accustomed to hearing about in fables and tall tales; who care for nothing more than the savagery of their bloodlust. Rather, the Altrinion-Vampires walk with such grace it almost appeared their feet barely touched the ground. And the wolves—the wolves were not rugged, tree-hugging beasts. They were demure, sophisticated, and alluring.

Having a front row seat to their world is a rarity among mortals. Lucky for me, my family is among the small and quaint faction of human nobility called the Regency. Only a few handpicked humans are intimately acquainted with the supernatural world. As such it is now our turn to

## Chapter One

host our annual charity cotillion which aids in keeping the peace and civility between the humans and supernaturals.

Not only aiding in blood drives to support rehabilitated Scourge Vampires, but the charity ball also brings the wealthiest of the human faction in our region together to donate their pledges to The Guardians—keepers and protectors of The Order of Altrinion. My father and others in the Regency feel that we've had little Guardian protection over the years and that makes us vulnerable. He hopes to change that with this year's cotillion.

Yet, even as I gaze out of the window, I know this year will be different. I am not the same child who stood under the watchful and wary arm of my father, I am a woman. With my twenty-fifth birthday coinciding with Christmas, I will finally see the supernatural world with a more mature vision. And with it, my expectancy has reached its peak.

With the cotillion held at our estate, my father charged me with overseeing every facet of the festivities. I've scrutinized every detail, auction item, menu selection and guest list with such a careful eye, I can only hope both my father and mother will be proud.

"Win," I hear Mother calling to me from the hallway. "Are you coming, darling? Ross and Rae are waiting for you in the kitchen. We're all waiting!" She exclaims in a tone sweet enough not to pester but poignant enough to know my moment of musing has expired.

"Yes, Mother I'm coming," I yell over my shoulder, wishing I could idle just a minute longer.

"Okay, well, don't dally. They've made quite a spread of all your breakfast favorites. You don't want it to go cold, dear." Mother's voice trails a bit from my door as she speaks and the loud clank of her heels against the wooden floors muffle her matter-of-fact tone.

Even though I am an adult, it is still Mother's expectation that I follow her words, which means I shouldn't be more than a step behind her. Without even seeing her, I can almost picture her hands clasped just above her girlishly tight waist with her thin chin lifted high as she strides through the hallway.

"Right behind you," I say as I quickly round the corner, taking a deep breath as I do and primping my posture.

Just as I cross the threshold of the kitchen, the smell of Belgian waffles, bacon, and eggs fills my nose. The flavorful aroma makes my stomach rumble louder than I'd like and my mother's eyes quickly cross mine with indifference. Thankfully, the jovial claps and shouts of my twin cousins bar the rebuking remark sure to follow Mother's chiding gaze.

*Chapter One*

Shifting my attention away from her, I work hard to ignore her reprimanding glare and search my cousin's gleeful faces for consolation. How thankful I am for the ever-jolly Merry & Pippin of my life. While it's unfortunate they lost their parents so young, having them living with us brought a light back into the halls of the manor.

*That light was snuffed out the day my brother Melchior died.*

Since then, I alone have served as both *daughter and son* to my parents. His loss was just that great.

"Happy Birthday, Win!" Ross and Rae shout in unison with their hands outstretched, offering me a seat at the table.

"Oh, you really didn't have to do all of this. Besides it's not my birthday until tomorrow," I respond as both cousins loop their arms through mine, ushering me to the table.

"I'd think a simple thank you would suffice," Mother says in her most scornfully syrupy tone.

"Well, we are more than happy to do this for you, Win." Rae slices her words straight through my mother's apparent disapproval. "And with the cotillion tonight and all the supers musing about the grounds, we'll hardly have time to give you a good and proper celebration. I'm sure having a birthday eclipsed by the most commercial time of the year gets tiresome. That's why Ross and I thought it best to make all your favorites."

"My sister is right, Win," Ross adds as he pours coffee into my favorite cup. "Today—well, at least this morning is our time to celebrate you. You do so much for us all, taking care of this manor—everything," Ross continues, flailing his arms with a bright smile. "It's time someone does something for you!"

Gazing up at my mother, I see even her hard-shell cracking as she allows a small smile to cross her face as she takes a seat opposite me. While I know she's not a fan of the twins bustling antics, even she can't help to be won by their charms.

"Fine! You two! Please don't make a fuss," I laugh as Ross and Rae kiss my cheeks and sitting themselves down at my sides. "Let's eat."

# Chapter Two

## *Lux*

"Brother, will you sit here sulking all day? Or do you plan to ready yourself for the festivities at Elysian Manor tonight?" My brother's gruff inquiry should bother me more, but I am strangely unmoved. I have no intention of stepping one foot into that ballroom tonight no matter his qualms.

"And what would you say if I just kept my attention to the flat screen? Everton hosts Manchester this afternoon and I have no desire to miss it," I reply, as I work to connect my phone's Bluetooth to the television so that I can cast the game.

"Luxor! This is important! Our presence, more than any is of upmost importance. Your attendance is not an option. Besides, you're a full member of the guard. You are expected to at least show your face," Cedric contests, positioning himself between me and the television.

"Don't antagonize him, my dear," my sister-in-law, Abigail begins. "You're only making matters worse."

"How am I making matters worse?" Cedric raves, tossing his hands in the air and looking over his shoulder at his wife who only chuckles and smiles in response.

"Heed your wife, brother," I quietly mutter, sliding opposite my brother to get a better view of the flat screen.

"Well, he's a Decanter man like you. Which means stubborn. The more you pester him, the more he'll resist," Abigail adds with a wink and nods to me over my brother's shoulder as she pours blood into a tall tumbler.

"Don't tell me Braelyn has you on the sippy cup thing too?" I tease, shaking my head.

"I must admit, it's not my preference but it's a better look among so many humans. I'll need to carry this around all day and sip just to keep my urges in control. Got to be on my best behavior," Abigail responds with a forced smile.

"And therein lies my discontent. All of this for the humans—and for what? What do we get out of it? Most just fancy the Altrinion Vampires so

## Chapter Two

much they barely notice the rest of us. Besides, I've yet to see why we must pretend to be something we're not for one night in front of a faction who are well aware of what we are. It's quite demeaning!" I protest, watchful of my brother's condemning glare.

"*Demeaning*? Really, Luxor? So, let me get this straight," Cedric starts. "You think it's demeaning to play dress up to gain the favor of the mortals but not demeaning to bare your nakedness before them and howl at the moon!"

"Exactly! It's not my fault, dear brother you aren't as comfortable with your own nakedness as I am. I mean you were born naked, were you not? Tell me, dearest sister-in-law, does he ever take his clothes off, or are you forced to mate between your tethered fabrics?"

Before I can blink my brother is wrestling me to the ground, pounding my face with two pillows from the loveseat. I can't help laughing at both his annoyance and anger toward me. While he's grown accustomed to my younger brother antics over the years, he draws the line when I tease his stoic and statue like style of romance. Wrong, I know, but I still like to goad him from time to time.

"Will you two stop it! You'll make a ruckus, and the humans will get nervous," Abigail shouts, swatting us both with the pillows.

Cedric remains on top of me, his heavy hands forcing my shoulders into the faux fur rug beneath us. I can't stop laughing but my brother's face has tensed, and I know his patience is waning.

"I will stop it if my little brother promises to join us tonight," Cedric seethes, his eyes glowing red.

"Fine! I call uncle! Uncle!" I laugh, trying to push my hands to his chest, but his hold on me is firm.

"Lux, can you please promise your brother you'll join us tonight? Please." The lilt in Abigail's tone is disturbing. "I can almost smell the humans startled fear from afar. I really can't have them coming to the suite right now. I haven't finished my tumbler and I'm famished. I'd hate to cause a scene so soon."

"Well, what say you?" Cedric demands, his eyes set on his wife's nervous smile and his hold on me lessens.

Pushing myself up from the floor, I know attending the festivities tonight is not only my obligation to the Guard, but to my family. I've long known my presence alone somehow sates both my brother and his wife's ravenous lust for blood. They need me. Even more, I too, need them, although I'd never admit it.

"I'll be there, brother," I say leaning against the sofa. "Besides, Manchester doesn't play for

## Chapter Two

another few hours. I'll have time to watch the game before the festivities. That is, after I take my leave for a run."

"A run? Brother, you can't be serious? There's been no wolf activity in this area in a while. If anyone sees you—"

"No worries, Cedric. No one will see me. I'm not going to hunt. Just a run. Between the boat ride to the island, the plane and the train—I need to stretch all four legs. The beast within is restless! I need to wolf out before you force me to play docile in the company of the domestics."

"Dearest, please. Let your brother go. I'm sure he has grown tired of playing third wheel in our little world. And you need to feed as well," Abigail softly says, wrapping her arm around Cedric's waist. He heaves a heap of air and smiles as she nuzzles into his neck. I respond with a sigh, fingering my hands through my hair. My sister-in-law is right, I do need a break from their constant cuddling, nor do I fancy smelling the gallons of blood it will take to sate their thirst enough to be around mortals tonight.

"All right, Luxor, just please be careful. You never know who you'll run into out there."

"Cedric, how many times must I ask you to call me Lux? Besides, whoever crosses my path will surely be a breath of fresh air compared to all the swooning I've had to endure as of late."

"Oh no! By all means stay, dear brother. We haven't even started swooning as you say. And you know what comes next? Kissing!" Cedric jeers, tossing a pillow at my feet.

"That's my cue! Anything but kissing!" I chuckle, throwing the pillow back at him and rush out the terrace door.

# Chapter Three

## *Winter*

"I am stuffed!" I say, leaning back into my chair, pulling at my belt buckle. "Thanks so much everyone! Everything was delicious. I really appreciate it."

"Oh, it was our pleasure, Win. But there's still so much more," Ross replies, heaping a large spoonful of fried apples on my plate.

"I'm full, really I am," I answer, pushing my plate away. Mother gives me an approving nod and eyewink before getting up from the table. Although I'm surprised she said nothing about all the sugary carbs I just inhaled, I know too well not to overindulge.

"Well, I'm sorry, Kharon, it looks as though we've missed a rather hearty breakfast," I hear my father say from the side door. Looking up to see my father's friendly smile warms my heart. But when he casts his gaze over his shoulders and I see Kharon, the warmth of my heart freezes cold.

"Thankfully, I am not here for the breakfast, Lord Elysian. I'm here for the birthday girl," Kharon answers in a gritty tone with a shifty smile to match.

Although almost every woman, including my cousin Rae, fancies our local wealthy ferryman, I do not see him as others do. Neither his wealth nor charisma impresses me. Nor do his strong jawline, crescent smile, deep gray eyes or dirty blonde hair entice me. He has never done anything but show interest in me, but it's my parents' overt interest in his interest towards me that curdles my bowels.

Kharon smiles wide as he comes to my father's side. Dressed impeccably as always, from his taut, fitted blue shirt to his athletic cut black trousers, his style alone is enough to impress Rae and all the women of the island. Even his copper logo medallion of a scorpion that he always wears with a leather cord around his neck, hangs perfectly against his chiseled physique. Still, it does nothing for me.

*Chapter Three*

"Please, come sit down, Kharon," Mother insists as she pulls a chair out for him near me. "There's plenty left. Come help yourself. And of course, you too my dear," she continues as my father dotes a peck on her cheek.

"Yes, do have some Uncle," Ross says in his normal bright tone. "I'm sure there is enough for you and your um—guest." Ross quickly sets plates in front of my father and Kharon and I sense his brightness fade.

"Ross, please. Mr. Nyx is no guest. Why, he's more like family. Is he not, Win?" My mother adds in a tepid tone, trying hard to hide her frustration of my cousin's newfound annoyance.

"Actually, my dear, I forgot I have some things to discuss with you. As a matter of fact, why don't we all give Win and Kharon a moment alone," my father says hurriedly, pushing back from the table. Before my mother has a chance to protest, he takes her hand and ushers her out of the kitchen. Snapping his fingers, the twins quickly follow but Ross gives me a tight glare, hunching his shoulders and he and Rae exit.

My eyes are still following my family's awkward departure when Kharon lets out a faux cough as his rough hands are still over mine. I gasp at his touch, realizing this is probably the first time I've felt his hands without gloves. Just as I imagined, nothing about him entices me and I slowly

*One Winters Kiss*

withdraw my hand to take a sip of my now cold coffee.

"Well," he starts with another forced throat clearing. "I hope this isn't as weird for you as it is for me, Win." Kharon's gray eyes deepen into mine and while I see his sincerity seeping through, it does nothing for me.

"A little weird, yes." I gulp my coffee down quick and grab a linen cloth to dab the corners of my mouth. "So, you came back from the shipyard earlier than usual?" I say trying to make this moment less bizarre.

"Ah yes, so you noticed?" Kharon's grin widens, and I realize I'm giving him the wrong impression. "With all the supernaturals in town for the ball, I thought it best to stay to land for the duration. But there's another reason I'm here."

"Oh?" I question as my eyes carefully scan the new nervousness now folding over his otherwise perfect face. He scratches his temples where a sliver of gray now edges his hairline and smiles back at me as his hand fidgets in his inside coat pocket.

"I suppose the reason your father left with the others is because he knows I wanted to—um—ask you something." As Kharon speaks my eyes grow wide as he pulls a small velvet box out. Although it looks tiny in his palm, it grows large in my mind. "Win, I know I've expressed interest in you over

## Chapter Three

the years but being as though I'm bound to a life at sea by trade, we've never really been able to get a real relationship off the ground. All of that changes now, with this."

Kharon's deep gray eyes are glassy but reminiscent of the sky after a storm. With his other hand he cups his palm with mine and takes a deep breath. An edge of sweat beads along his brow but he keeps his gaze set on me, gleaming his perfect smile.

"Kharon, I don't know—we—well—um—I don't—"

"Please, don't say anything yet. I care for you deeply, Win. I always have and I always will. I've spoken to your father, and he knows of my affection for you. And I know there's an ocean between us—well, age wise. But having married a younger woman himself, Lord Elysian understands. I spent the better part of my youth harnessing my skills and building my business. But the time has come for me to make more important things priority. Like family. And it all begins with you. No, I misspoke. With us."

My mouth is locked, and I sense desire now deepening in Kharon's longing gaze as his eyes flutter to the rise and fall of my cleavage as I heave gulps of air. The strength of his hand intensifies, and I feel him coming closer.

Even more I feel the room closing in around us.

A loud crash behind me breaks our forming silence and Kharon's eyes dart darkly over my shoulder.

Ross and Rae are both standing at the archway of the kitchen with their mouths gaped open. A small teacup lays broken at Rae's feet and Ross's eyes lock with mine in disbelief.

"Oh my, we're so very sorry about making such a ruckus!" Ross says walking toward me and Kharon. "We're such gufflebups sometimes, really. Well, more my twin than me, but gufflebups just the same."

"Guffle—what?" Kharon questions annoyed, covering the velvet box with his hand as he watches Ross coming closer, breaking up his intended tender moment. "Well, actually, we were in the middle of so—"

"I know and I certainly do apologize. But Stephen at the lumber yard just called. It appears, dear cousin we failed to mark up the last pinelings for dispatch. And well, you know those broody lumbermen—won't chop a tree unless it's marked quite right. Right? So we should get going. Besides there's bears and such in the forests these days, best to get going while we have those burly jacks at our behest. I'm so sorry, Mr. Nyx but being a businessman, I'm quite sure you understand," Ross says, looping his arm through mine and tugging me through the side door.

*Chapter Three*

"But, Win, we still have things to discuss!" Kharon shouts to our backs, now in the doorway.

"Discuss them with Rae! I'm sure she'll be delighted!" Ross yells back over his shoulder with a chuckle.

"*Thank you!*" I mouth to Ross, leaning into his lanky shoulder as we rush down the snowy walkway.

"My pleasure, dear cousin." Ross examines my faces as he stops short of the pine tree fields, biting his lip.

"What is it, Ross? Come on, spit it out! I know you're dying to say something," I say, knowing the minute he sunk his teeth into his bottom lip, he's holding back a mouthful.

"Was that little velvet box what I think it was?" He questions, shoving a thick layer of snow off the bench at the end of the cobblestone pathway. Taking off his coat and placing it on the marble slab he gestures for me to take a seat.

"I have no idea. Well, he never got an opportunity to open it when you showed up."

"Well, what else could it be? The man has had you in his sights since the day you turned twenty-one," Ross keeps his eyes set with mine, likely hopeful for more of a response but a sigh is all I have in reply. "I mean you know Rae fancies him, right? I suppose I should say Rae and almost every woman on the island."

"Every woman except me. As I've told Rae before she's more than welcome to him and his obvious daddy-kink fantasies. I have no need to oblige. I'm not looking for a daddy—I already have one. A partner—my fairytale prince, however, to share my life—that's what I want—well, that is, when I've taken time to live a life."

"I hate to say I doubt you'll find any such Prince Charming on this forsaken icicle! Not unless you have your eyes set on the guys from the lumberyard. Just be sure it's not Stephen—I've called dibbs!" Ross laughs with a small jab to my ribs. He stands from the bench and stretches as he looks around the snow. "By now I'm sure you know I only said Stephen needed us to come tag the pinelings. The truth is he did ask, and I did so oblige—alone, with him last night." A small, shy smile covers my cousin's slender face as red blushes his otherwise toffee coated cheeks while he laughs.

And while everything in me wants to inquire further about his time alone with Stephen last night in the pine fields, I am more fearful of the large black bear now approaching Ross from behind. Ross's chuckle subsides and his smile fades as he senses the looming presence at his rear. Father has always taught us to be careful in the fields. Normally one of the lumbermen are near or I'd have my holster. Not today.

*Chapter Three*

Today the error of running out on Kharon may prove to be my downfall. I know better not to be so reckless—but here I am. My hands lock into the marble bench as Ross stands frozen before me. Fear minces with the crisp wintry air and I almost forget to breathe as my mouth falls open in panic. Slowly, the bear stands from all fours, towering over both Ross and the Christmas trees at our sides. The bear releases a loud roar and dread strikes my heart. Before I can react, a menacing growl rises from the side of the bench and a large dark grey wolf emerges from between the thick pine brush. His golden eyes meet with mine and although I know I should be afraid, the pacing of my heart lessens, and I instantly feel safe. And perhaps, *something more.*

# Chapter Four

*Lux*

I've never been so eager to phase than I am right now, but the wolf restrains me. Everything in me wants to shift into human form and learn more about this mortal woman who now catches my heart. Just the sweet smelling, albeit fretful breath she exhaled at the sight of the carnivorous beast before her is enough to lure me to her side.

At this moment being a hybrid, half-Altrinion and half-wolf has its perks. Most wolves are overtaken in their wolf form they cannot separate the lycanthropic power of their wolf from their supernaturality. As such they would normally take no interest in a human, beautiful or otherwise.

If I've never been thankful to be a hybrid before, I am this day.

I'd sure hate to pass on any moment in her presence. Ever.

Still, the wolf reins over my lustful inhibitions as he lets out another cautionary rumble, warning the black bear to take his leave. The bear growls back, but I sense he means no harm, despite his posturing. Although to humans he appears an adult, his scent tells me he is only an adolescent. He roars once more as he lowers to his forelegs, hitting the lanky companion of the Lovely Woman. As he does, the young man falls, hitting his head on the marble bench, rendering him unconscious.

My wolf snarls in frustration, knowing the bear intentionally hit the young man. He wants the humans to know he could cause more pain if he wanted. Growling low in response, I let him know his point is made, insisting he moves on. As he shuffles through the snow his paws pound the ground beneath him. He's too young to fully stomp walk to mark the territory, but seeing me, he likely wants to ward off any other wolves. Being Altrinion, I'm larger than the average sized wolf and I'm sure he doesn't wish to have more of my kind in his territory.

"Ross!" The Lovely Woman screams, turning my attention away from the bear and back to her. The scent of fresh spilled blood hits my nose

*Chapter Four*

before I see the small bruise on the back of her companion's head. Falling to her knees, she turns him on his side, examines his wounds and tries to wake him.

*I need to help her.*

Normally, I would not do this in front of a human unless it was absolutely necessary. This seems necessary. Before I have a moment to talk myself out of it, I let out one yelping roar and shift back to human form.

Looking up at me from the ground, her eyes grow wide with the fullness of my manhood directly in her view. Thankfully, a sliver of the sun's light rests between us and she peers up at me beneath her small palm rested above her brow. Still, a passionately primal part of me could linger here just a minute longer. But I know better.

*Help her, idiot.*

"Let's get him off the cold ground. If he has a concussion, the cold will make it worse," I say dropping to one knee at her side. While she keeps her hands on her companion's shoulders, she hasn't taken her eyes off me and for that I am grateful.

But she is not the only one.

It's actually hard for me to pay attention to anything or anyone other than her. Gazing at her full luscious lips makes me want to crush my mouth to hers with neither permission nor regret.

Her small, oval face is blemish free as her perfectly cocoa-covered complexion glistens beneath the dewy snow resting on her skin.

Goodness, she is perfect!

I've never seen a mortal, or supernatural as gorgeous as this lovely creature before me.

Instantly, memories of the stories my brother Cedric told me of how he knew he was meant to be with his beloved, Abigail, from the second he first saw her flood my thoughts. Until the day he saw her, a dire Scourge in the taming halls of the Civility Center, he never made no pledge to endow his lycanthropy and run with me as a wolf. Instead, whatever strange magic took hold of his heart that night led him to turn to his Altrinion nature and sate his vampiric thirst of blood for no other reason than to aid in her taming.

Because as he said, he loved her from the first day their eyes met.

Never have I thought such a notion to override my intellect, but here I am, lost in the lure of this Lovely Woman.

"Perhaps you should cover yourself before someone sees you," she says, breaking my lovesick musing. "Here, take this," she continues, handing me a coat from the bench.

"Are you not afraid?" I question, taking the thin coat from her and wrapping it around my waist. She works hard to modestly avert her eyes, but

*Chapter Four*

she keeps her periphery set on me. Her lips crinkle as I tunic the cottony fabric into a knot at my sides, likely annoyed I'm not putting it on. "I doubt it'll fit," I say answering the question she's too reserved to ask.

"Oh, of course!" She answers resolutely, swallowing hard and looking back down to her companion. "And no, I'm not afraid," she adds, this time more staunch. Lifting her companion's head slightly under her hands, her expression softens as her big brown eyes drift back up to my own. "You're not the first supernatural I've ever met—well perhaps the first without clothes," she says with a sheepish smile.

Returning her attention to the young man, it takes everything in me not to wrap my arms around her and make her mine in every way imaginable. But I know better. Besides, it's not a good thing for me to remain as I am, lest someone come.

"We should probably get him out of the cold now. Is there somewhere I can take him for you?" I question, lifting her companion from the cold ground, cradling him in my arms. For a rather long-limbed guy, he's heavier than his small frame suggests. The Lovely Woman regards me with a smile, and I see my actions please her and I want to do nothing more than to cement that beautiful smile on her face.

"If you'll follow me, there's a log cabin just on the other side of the tree line. It'll be the most private place today since the lumbermen are out on deliveries."

"Private is good." A low growl escapes me. I know my wolf is as pleased as I am—perhaps, even more so. Although I wish nothing more than to be alone with this woman, I'll take what I can get for now.

*And I plan to take it all.*

## Chapter Five

*Winter*

Once we're in the cabin my wolfen stranger lays Ross on the bed in the back room as I quickly grab a cool towel and lay over the small bump on his head. Thankfully, he's not bleeding anymore but I know he needs a little time to rest.

As we make our way into the front den, butterflies swarm inside me as the deep gaze of my new companion sears parts of me that have never been awaken until now. Even the quietness sitting between us builds things in me I've never felt before.

But I can't take my eyes off of him.

Quickly lighting the wood in the fireplace, I try to distract myself from enjoying gawking too long.

This cabin feels too small for him. Even though large, burly lumbermen usually make camp here managing our pine fields, they seem small in comparison to the six foot plus wonder now before me. His caramel-coated bronzed frame takes up the doorway to the room where he just laid Ross.

What's worse is that it is taking everything within me to keep my eyes above his waistline as my cousin's coat does little to hide the embodiment of his masculinity beneath.

"There are clothes in the wardrobe," I say turning my back and pointing over my shoulder when I spy more than an eyeful of the wonderfulness of him. Being a virgin, I've never seen a man before and this is not how I expected it to go---but it is certainly more than I could ever imagine. "The lumber men aren't as um—big as you, but I'm sure something should fit. I'd hate for you to catch a cold."

"That is very thoughtful of you. Thank you." His response is soft, but his words strangely seem to meet my ears despite him standing such a distance from me.

A loud, rippling wind rushes through the cabin and I turn to find my wolfen stranger now fully clothed before me. My breath hitches as I'm brought in full view of his chiseled chest peeking

*Chapter Five*

behind the tightly fitted plaid shirt. A pair of cargo pants with suspenders almost adequately fit his frame while still leaving some of his waist exposed, sending my abandoned thoughts into a frenzy.

"Um—that was fast," I say, looking around the cabin, trying not to get lost in the lure of him.

"Please, tell me, what is your name?" he asks, lifting my chin to meet his eyes.

"Everyone calls me Win," I whisper, almost breathless as his golden, wide eyes stare into mine.

"Ah," he begins, and the coolness of his breath prickles my pores. "So, is that your name or is that what everyone calls you? Is it short for something? Winona—or something like that?" His gaze deepens and his hold on my chin firms.

"No, well—um, it's short for Winter. But everyone calls me Win for short."

"And do you prefer Win? What shall I call you, my lovely lady?" As he speaks his thumb strums the corners of my mouth and I can't help the release of my jaw at his touch.

"Winter," I breathe, pressing my face into his palm as his large hands spread, cradling my head.

"Then Winter it shall be. Tell me, Winter, is there a story behind your name?" With this inquiry he slowly releases his hold and trails his hands down my arms, clasping my hands into his.

A small chuckle escapes me at his questioning as I think of the best way to respond. "Well, my parents met when my father was fifty. After his first wife passed, he met my mother who was only twenty-one. Mother said it was a whirlwind romance and they married just weeks after they met. I came along not far behind. He chose my name because he said I was born in his winter season. I suppose being born on Christmas solidified his choosing."

"Oh, so tomorrow is your birthday! I hope I'm not keeping you from any celebrations, Winter." A lilt of concern rings through his tone and his brows tense.

"No, you're not. My family made me a big breakfast."

"Anything else? What are you doing to culminate the grand occasion?" His smile broadens with a hint of concern drifting between his brows.

"Who me? Um—I don't know. My birthday is usually eclipsed by all things Christmas and Boxing Day, I normally just squeeze in time with family then it's back to business as usual. Between managing the cotillion, Elysian Manor, and the pine fields for Christmas there isn't much time left for celebrating."

"That's not good, Winter. You should be celebrated. On your birthday and every day."

"I suppose, but—"

"But nothing. That changes now."

*Chapter Five*

I can't help bursting with laughter at his sentiment. Falling into a wooden rocker near the fireplace and covering my mouth I am amused at his forwardness. His brow raises and a sexy smirk forms on his perfect face and everything in me knows he's sincere.

Scooting a small leather chair close to me, he sits and grins once more. "Why are you laughing, Winter?"

"I suppose I'm wondering how you can declare such a thing when you know nothing about me save my name. I don't even know yours. All I know about you is you're a wolf."

"Ah, I see. Fair point. My name is Lux—short for Luxor. My surname, Decanter. I shortened it to Lux and have preferred to be called such since Vegas threw up that monstrosity of a casino eons ago. I have no desire to be likened to it in any way. Also, to clarify, you're partly correct. I am a wolf—but I am so much more."

The grace of his speech is refreshing compared to the grisly men I've grown accustomed to on the island. He is every bit as dashing as I recall of his kind.

"Hold on, what do you mean more?"

"I thought I wasn't the first supernatural you've met?" Leaning back, he smiles as his eyes loom full of curiosity. All I can do is hunch my shoulders in response and his smile widens. He appears happy to share. "Well, I'm sure you've heard of Altrinions. I am half-Altrinion and half wolf. It makes me a bit different than most wolves. I can change at will, not restricted to the full moon only. Hybrids like me don't have to posture as normal pack wolves for alpha status. We can choose our lot, unlike the others. Most important, I had a choice."

"To be Altrinion or Wolf?" I ask.

"Yes, and you can see the choice I made," Lux responds sitting up in the chair, and moving closer to me. "Now, my lovely Winter, I'd like to talk to you about your choices. For starters, do you, in fact, have any interest in the lumbermen here as your companion suggested? I do need an answer, so that I can know to whom I must dispatch because I don't think I can see anyone at your side except me, both now and always. I'd hate to move heaven and earth to prove my point, but if I must, I shall."

Gasps erupt through me at his admission, and I feel the pace of my heart quicken. I care not how he knows my discussion with Ross. Instead, I am more surprised that I am in full agreement.

# Chapter Six

*Lux*

The sweet coolness of her breath lingers upon my skin, delighting me with a fervor I've never known until now. Her lusciously gaping mouth is indeed the most enticing thing I've ever seen and it's taking the full strength of my will to override my impulse to make myself one with her in this instant.

Still, I need an answer and I need it now. I will not act upon my desires without knowing if there is someone else.

"So, Winter, please tell me. Is there someone else?" I question and her eyes fall to her hands as she fidgets with the thick crease of her riding pants. Placing my hand over hers, I still her twitching and her gaze slowly retreats back to mine.

She forms her mouth to answer but a bout of defiance brews between her brows and her lips curl as her eyes narrow and she pulls her hand from mine.

"Wait a minute! How do you know about my conversation with my cousin Ross? You were in wolf form when we first saw you. Were you lurking around somewhere? Spying on us? If so, why?" Winter's words roll from her lips in a flurry and her scent tells me she's wary of me.

I need to fix this.

"No need to worry, sweetness. I can assure you I was not spying on you. I was out for a run when I came upon you and your—um, cousin—well, at least my second question is answered. Now, if you will, back to my first," I reply, cupping her hand in mine once more.

*It feels great holding her.* Even if it's just her hand.

"That still doesn't explain how you were able to hear us. I thought wolves were purely in animal-only mode while in phase—that your human part went to sleep. None of this makes sense." While I know she's still slightly cautious, I am thankful she doesn't retract her hand again.

"Altrinion hybrid wolves such as me aren't your run of the mill breed. We're different. We live

*Chapter Six*

dually as both Altrinion and wolf. That is how I was able to hear you. Now, are you going to answer me or should I just go about bringing your entire enclave of lumbermen to their end. I'd hate to do so, being the Eve of Christmas and all. But if I must be the Grinch, I will. If only it means you will be mine."

"Be yours?"

"Yes, Winter. Mine. *All mine.* So tell me, please."

"There's—um—there's nothing to tell. I have no interest in any of the lumbermen or any other man for that matter," she quietly answers, and her eyes go distant.

"I see."

"Well, not that I'm not interested in men—well, not any of the men here. I mean—you're here—but—"

"I think I know just what you mean, sweetness."

"What then—um—about you?"

"No. I'm not interested in any men here either," I laugh, and she joins as well, tossing her hands to her mouth. "My apologies for teasing, but you are just so cute and tempting. I couldn't resist."

The words hang in the silence between us, and she pants passionately, mesmerizing me by the rise and fall of her curvaceous cleavage.

"Well, then don't. Don't resist, Lux." Her eyes darken and I spy the makings of a delectable vixen peering through her otherwise round, innocent brown eyes. Fluttering her thick lashes, she scans the length of me, and her lips wander open once more and I can no longer stifle the urge to acquiesce her request.

Reaching my hand around the small of her neck, raking my fingers through her soft, curly tendrils, I pull her close to me. Searching her face for even a hint of disapproval, I find none. Everything in her face and the scent of passion pouring from her pores is saying *Yes* to me.

Still, I'll not plant my mouth to hers without permission. I need to hear her say it.

"Winter, may I kiss you?"

Desire builds between us as the fusing of our pheromones mix as one molecule in the air we now share.

"Yes," she breathes, leaning her head into my palm and the magnetism of her longing stare pulls me to the precipice of passion. I know if I let the beast within me have his way, I'd rip her clothes from her body and glory in the revelation of her nakedness. But she deserves better.

This is more than sex. Dare I say more than passion? She is both my mate and my love. I want to explore every inch of her, learning each hill and valley intimately. I want to know her dreams, cares, wants and needs. I want to be not only what she needs but who she needs. I want to discover her depths and peruse her peaks. Everything she is I want to partake.

*Chapter Six*

And I will willingly give her all of me.

Looking into her eyes, I can say I have finally found the ominous thing that has long evaded me.

*Love.*

"Where shall I kiss you, Winter?" I ask, hopeful for permission to be set free here and now, planting my mouth over the entirety of her.

"Please, Lux, kiss my lips," she pants, closing her eyes in anticipation.

Just as the words escape her, my mouth is locked to her lips. The sweetness of her tongue, like brown sugar and maple, makes me zealous for more. As our tongues swirl as one, her effervescence hits my nose, sending me into a frenzy. Winter pulls me closer as her hands rest at my back, moving along my muscles, locking our bodies together like magnets.

Slowly as I can, I suck at her bottom lip, sampling her sweet nectar while gently releasing my hold. Chuckling, a small smile creeps over her face and she shyly cups her hands over her mouth.

"Why are you laughing, sweetness? I hope our kiss wasn't that bad."

"No, of course not. I'm sorry. I guess it's just that was my first kiss—ever." The innocence of her wide eyes as she stares at me, makes my heart melt. Now I intend to be her first of many. *And her only.*

# CHAPTER SEVEN

## *WINTER*

Not only am I surprised that I just had my first kiss with a stranger, but I am even more surprised this stranger does not feel like a stranger at all. There is a comfort in the familiarity I have with him that seems impossible.

"Well, Winter, I must say I am both honored and intrigued," Lux says, taking my hands in his, resting it over his heart.

"Intrigued?" I question, looking up at his sun-spun eyes.

"Yes. Intrigued because I cannot believe a woman of your beauty, grace, and charm has yet to be kissed. Don't get me wrong, I am honored for the privilege. I don't think I can stomach any other lips touching yours but mine. I hope that's okay."

"Oh! Wow—I—um—don't know what to say, but it's a bit forward, don't you think?" I feel like I must say something, even though the truth is, I don't mind what he said.

"I suppose it could seem so. I admit I've never thought like this before. My older brother Cedric always teases that I am not patient or disciplined enough for love. Never until now have I ever wanted to be under love's control—but you—you bring out something in me I never thought a wretched soul like me capable."

Mother has always taught me not to be one of those loose women who drops her virtue like a tattered rag. And for years I have not. I've had my share of men who have sought to court me, including Kharon, but never have I been so willing to reciprocate. Until now.

"It is strange, I know. My mind keeps saying, *Winter this is too much too soon*—but I know I've never felt like this before. How do I know it's not just some fleeting feeling of lust? You know because I saw you naked! And what of tomorrow? What happens when you return to from wherever you came?"

"No, Winter!" Lux begins, lifting me in his arms and placing me on his lap. Taking my chin in his

## Chapter Seven

hand, he kisses my lips softly once more and smiles. "Have no fear for tomorrow. I have no intention in the storybook of you and me ending with one winter's kiss. For there shall be seasons of sweet springs, sensual summers, amorous autumns, and wondrous winters for us to behold. Together."

"But we don't know anything about each other," I quietly respond, trailing my hand across his chest. The thumping of his heart syncs with the pacing of my own and I am impressed even our biorhythms are in harmony.

This is all so much so fast. But I love it.

"What more would you like to know?" He questions, brushing my hair to the side so he can get a full view of my face.

"Everything," I answer, combing my hands through his wavy brown hair. Long tendrils fall adjacent to his cheekbone and his thick brows are perfectly sculpted, highlighting his entrancing eyes. Sporting a five o'clock shadow, his squared jawline is chiseled making his currant covered lips even more inviting.

"Win," I hear Ross's piercing voice cut into Lux's response just as he forms his lips to speak.

"I should check on my cousin," I say, lightly kissing the crown of Lux's head. Pressing his lips tight, he smiles then tilts his head toward the room, gesturing for me to see to Ross.

"Win," Ross cries out once more.

"I'm here, Ross," I answer. Ross looks around the room bewildered but smiles slightly as I sit at his side. "No worries, cousin, you're okay."

"The—the bear—what happened?" Ross chatters his words as he winces, touching the forming knot on his head.

"The bear is gone, but you'll be just fine."

"But how? Win?"

"Well, we were rescued. We had a little help."

"Help? Huh? I don't understand," Ross answers, confused.

"This should help," Lux says standing at the threshold of the room and hands me another cool towel. A smile is all I offer for my appreciation, and he nods back, smiling.

"Win, who is that? Is it Stephen?" Ross questions trying to see over my shoulder, but his eyes close in apparent exhaustion and he drifts back asleep.

"Winter, do you mind if I offer some assistance?" Lux asks. Without waiting for my reply, he makes his way to Ross's side and kneels down, placing two fingers on his wrist to test his pulse. "His pulse is faint," Lux says now leaning closer to listen to Ross's heart. He opens Ross's right eye and takes a long look into his irises. "I think he has a concussion. Do you mind?" Lux holds his hands over Ross's head and looks up at me, once more awaiting my reply.

## Chapter Seven

"Please, of course." I quickly answer, worry filling me. I inwardly berate myself for getting so lost in this moment with a stranger that I neglected to tend to my cousin.

Biting my fingernails, I watch as a warm, golden light shines from Lux's hands as he hovers them above Ross's head. Placing his hands over the bump on his head, I watch in awe as it subsides and a pulsing yellow glow beams through Ross's entire body.

"Oh my! Are you healing him?" I ask in shock and Ross tilts his head and rolls over on his side.

"I just need a little nap, Stephen," Ross coos with a quaint smile, pulling the blanket up to his chin and nuzzling deeper into the bed.

"I suppose he really likes this Stephen, huh?" Lux stands and smiles, kissing my forehead. "He should be fine in a little while, let's give him some privacy in the event those dreams become too intense."

"Wow," I begin as Lux leads us out of the room and onto the loveseat opposite the fireplace. "Looks like I've learned a lot more about you, Mr. Decanter. Any more tricks up those plaid sleeves of yours?"

"Nope. No tricks, sweetness, but I am eager to learn more about the only woman to ever see me in plaid, and the only one to ever do so again. But I need more, Winter. No, I misspoke. *I need all.*"

# Chapter Eight

*Lux*

Winter is far more relaxed than she was initially. More than an hour has passed since our first kiss, and I've learned quite a bit about her.

She is Winter Elysian. Daughter of Lord Elysian; leader of the mortal faction of the Regency.

Also, I know she has never spent much time away from the island. Loves riding horses. Chiefly, her favorite, Mr. Puddles. She hates fish—notably the smell of it. Something about most men of the island reeking of it was particularly of interest and quite amusing. Also, I now know she and her twin cousins are very close. By the way she's checked in on Ross intermittently, I can tell just how much they mean to her.

"Listen to me ramble! I'm sorry, Lux. I'm sure you have better things to do than hear about my machinations with my cousins, my time managing the estate, and putting together this year's cotillion," Winter says, once more fidgeting with the crease along her pants.

"No, I've enjoyed it, really. But what about you? You've told me of all the planning you put into the cotillion, how busy you are managing the estate, and who you care for in your family but what of your aspirations or dreams. Desires?"

"Don't you think that's a mouthful for one day, Lux?" Winter questions, looking up at me through her thick lashes.

"Hardly. Tell me, you're turning twenty-five tomorrow, what is it that you want to do? Do you want to keep managing the manor or will you leave it in the hands of your brother?"

"My brother?" Her eyes glass as she stares up at me with a pain-staked face. "What do you know of my brother?" She adds with her head tilted just above her shoulder.

"I was here about a decade ago. I met Melchior then. At the time I thought for sure your father entrusted the care of the manor to him."

"You met Melchior? I—I don't understand," she asks, her tone fueled by both confusion and worry.

## Chapter Eight

"Yes, at the last cotillion. It is common for nobles such as your father to introduce their heirs to supernatural regency. Helps keep everything civil. Melchior was very kind—every bit as your father generous, I recall. I remember him fondly. I'd hoped to see him tonight. Although I did not know he had a sister at the time. I suppose he—"

"He's dead." Winter's grief-stricken words hang hauntingly between us. I've wanted to know everything about her, but this is not what I expected.

"Dear, Winter, please accept my apology. I had no idea. The kindness of your beloved brother has no equal among mortal men. Or supernatural."

"Thank you, Lux. I am sorry. I didn't mean to just throw it out there. It's just so painful," Winter confesses as tears flood her face. Taking my palm, I wipe her face and she presses her head into my hand. She exhales and pushes herself up on the sofa and tries to force a smile.

"You've had to do that a lot, haven't you?"

"Do what?"

"Feign happiness where sadness is yet apparent." Winter swallows hard at my words and looks up at the ceiling, batting her lashes, trying to stop the spillage of her tears. "You don't have to do that with me, Winter. Please, lean on me. Cry on my shoulder if you must. But don't you dare hold anything in. Not with me."

"It's just hard, Lux. I was still very young when he died. Not long after the last cotillion. It was an accident. Shipwrecked by a storm while looking for some rare treasure or something. I don't really know. We never recovered his body. His grave is empty save the tulips we placed in his coffin. They were his favorite flower. Everything changed that day. I became both son and daughter to my parents. Melchior was a product of Father's first marriage, the son he always wanted. He was a great big brother. Protective of me to a fault. I am sure he wouldn't be happy to learn my parents have made me step into his footsteps while side stepping my own. But he is not here to protest."

"No, he may not be here, but you now have me. And I shall protest to whatever is opposite your desires, my beautiful lady. What is it that you want to do? While I'm sure Lord Elysian means well, I have a feeling if he knew your interests lied elsewhere, he'd be more than happy to oblige. I'd be more than happy to motivate him to that end should it become necessary."

"Oh no! Please, Lux that isn't necessary. I know Father loves me. Besides, it's not his fault I never completed my last semester in school. He became ill and I had to come back to take care of things."

"I see. And what were you studying?" I question, trying to lighten the mood as I take her hand in mine.

## Chapter Eight

"Education. I did get my bachelor's, but I was working on my graduate degree."

"That's amazing, Winter! So you want to be a teacher? What subject?"

"I know it may sound far reaching but I actually want to open a school." She answers with a smile bright enough to force away her sadness.

"Oh that's not far reaching at all. It's actually quite impressive. What type of school?" I ask, now lured by the brightened smile now forcing aside her earlier melancholy.

"Growing up, a noble's daughter—it was tough. Knowing of the supernatural world but forbidden to engage in it. At least not until times like now where I've become of age. I can say my parents did their best with me and Melchior as well as Ross and Rae, but the other children are not so fortunate."

"How so?"

"Imagine going to regular school but with the burdened privilege of knowing there's more out there. The factions of families try to educate us but dare I say they're doing a poor job. Until today I never knew there were hybrid wolves or that you were capable of whatever healing ability you performed on Ross. Most fear the supernaturals too much to ask more or they're clueless altogether."

*One Winters Kiss*

"Ah, I see, so you want them to learn more about the supernatural world."

"Yes. That and of course common subjects like science, math and literature—and all the rest."

"Wow, Winter! That is amazing. I knew you were a remarkable woman, but this is so much more. I love your idea too. It's practically perfect."

*"Practically?"* Her brow raises and I can see she's almost insulted.

"Don't get me wrong, sweetness but there appears to be something missing." I reply, brushing her hair from her face so I can study what she looks like perturbed.

"Oh really? Well then, what would you suggest? You know to turn it from practically perfect to perfectly perfect." Winter crinkles her nose as she speaks, and I can tell she's trying hard not to be offended by making light of my comment. I take special note of her defensive strategies, lest I find myself in the doghouse one day.

"Winter, please know this is just an observation—not a suggestion."

"Out with it!" She huffs with her arms folded, now leaning back into the sofa and slightly away from me.

"Well imagine a class about Black people never taught by Black people or had Black people in the class. Or a French class taught by someone who doesn't speak the language? Do you think the

*Chapter Eight*

discussion might be missing an important member?"

"Oh," she answers quietly. Her eyes fall briefly, but she gazes back up at me and smiles. "That's actually a great idea, Lux! I guess I never thought about it. I mean, I never really think of supernaturals as children. I don't think I ever knew there were children."

"How do you think I got here?" I laugh and she does too, covering her mouth like she does and it's the cutest thing I've ever seen. Why she insists on hiding her lovely smile, I'll never know. "Yes, Winter, I too was a child once. So are most supernaturals. We are born. Now, Scourge Vampires are the only who are bitten. But at some point, they too, were children—just not vampires. The rest of us, Altrinions, Wolves, Bulwarks, we are all born just like every other created thing."

"But wait a minute—you said you knew Melchior. Based on your description of him you must've been an adult when you met him. *How old are you?*"

"Ah, so we're back to the topic of me, I see." Now I'm nervous. The fact she wasn't aware until now of the existence of my kind tells me she knows very little of the lifespan of a supernatural. While we aren't immortal—that's a word Hollywood gives to anything longer than a human's shelf life, we do progress slower than mortals.

Winter's eyes remain locked with mine and her straight seated posture tells me she expects an answer soon. She deserves one. It will break me if my age is a deal breaker for her, but I won't give up too easily.

Unless she tells me to do so.

Little does she know her words can either bind us together or break us apart. Her words have more power than she knows. Still, there's no need to put off the inevitable.

Swallowing the thick air in my throat, I decide it's now or never. "Two-hundred and ninety-two."

Her mouth falls open at my admission and I fear she will run away. What will be the result of my confession? I have no idea how she'll respond. *Until I do.*

Rising to her knees, she corners me between the throw pillows. Smiling, she brushes my hair away from my eyes and crushes her mouth to mine. I'll take this type of response every day. That is, of course, what I intend to do.

# Chapter Nine

## *Winter*

Surprisingly, the notion of Daddy-kink or a silver fox never enters my mind as I lock my lips tight with Lux's luscious, raspberry-hued lips. The tantalizing taste of his tongue swirling and locking with mine sends my hormones in overdrive.

Never in my life have I been this impetuous or overtaken by any man. Ever.

But this Altrinion hybrid wolf sends the dutiful and orderly woman my parents raised me to become aside. In this moment all I want is him. As his hands guide along the length of my back, all I can do is pant in his embrace, willing to throw all caution to the wind and will my innermost parts to him and him alone.

"My, my, Winter," Lux moans, slowly unlocking himself from our kiss. "That is certainly not the response I expected, but appreciatively the one I wanted." Laughing, I cover my face, looking over my shoulder, slightly embarrassed at the woman I've become in a stranger's arms. But nothing about him feels like a stranger to me. "No need to be shy now, my sweet. At least not in my arms," he adds with a sly smile while nestling me firmer in his lap.

His eyes darken as a lust-fueled grunt escapes me when I feel his protrusion at my bottom. "Lux," I moan as he presses me deeper into his hold. "I have something to confess," I say while resting my forehead to his, enjoying the feel of his arms around me.

"I am no priest, by any means, but please share what you will," he breathes back, and the coolness of his breath prickles my pores.

"I have never—um—I'm still a—"

"A virgin?" He completes my sentiment with a sly smile of satisfaction.

"Yes," I mumble with butterflies swelling within me.

Lux's sun-spun eyes flash with lustful delight and his now curved smile spans the entirety of his perfect face. Planting a quick, soft kiss on my lips, he keeps his head pressed with mine as he takes a deep breath. "And so you shall remain," he answers with a strained tone.

*Chapter Nine*

At his words, the warmth escapes me, leaving me cold inside.

"What?" I whisper, pushing myself out of his hold.

I am off his lap faster than I thought myself possible, backing away trying to stop shame from swallowing me whole. Even with my back now to the fireplace, nothing but chills erupt over me as I realize how much of a fool I must seem.

Jumping up from the sofa, the dulling glare etched on Lux's face is hard to miss. Exhaling hard, he paces the length of the couch, and I can't help but notice how the steel framed imprint of his manhood remains. If nothing more, at least I know for sure I was getting to him just as much as he was for me.

In that I find a modicum of pleasure.

"Please, Winter, let me explain," Lux begins with his hands raised in protest as he takes careful steps toward me.

"No, there's no need. I've already made a fool of myself! Besides, I think it's time for you to go so I can see about my cousin!" I bite back.

"I am sorry if my words disturbed you. Really, I am." I am almost impressed how Lux manages to remain calm. The sincerity of his tone is luring, but I refuse to let him pull me back in.

"You should go." My words are desperate. I don't know how much longer I can keep my wits about me with him staring at me as he does. From the protrusion yet glaring beneath his khakis to his sculpted chest peering behind the plaid outlining his decadence, it's all I can do to stand firm.

"If you would but let me explain," he pleads, inching closer, yet keeping enough of a distance so that I can't throw myself back into his embrace. His eyes search mine with caution, but his deep gaze cuts through the iciness forming around my heart.

"There's nothing to say, Lux!" I exclaim, turning my attention to the growing fire at my side, averting my eyes from his entrancing glare. Swallowing the hard air knotted in my throat, I lean into my father's stubbornness. "You need to leave!" I've dug my heels in and the daggered eye stare I shoot toward Lux meets him just as I intended.

For a moment, I watch as his eyes fall at my sentiment, but the newly defiant smirk etched across his face tells me he has no plans to oblige. "No!" He calmly resists. "Not until you hear me out."

Everything in me tells me to just let down my guard, that I am safe with him. But with exception to my father, my cousin Ross, and my departed brother, I have a natural distrust of men. Even more, Mother raised no fool. She taught me to be strong. Shrewd even if I must. I allowed lust to

## Chapter Nine

override my intellect for long enough in the arms of this stranger.

*Although he doesn't feel like a stranger to me.*

"Make it quick," I grit through my teeth, working hard to maintain my stance. Looking me over, Lux almost seems disappointed, but takes in a deep breath and leans against the mantle over the fireplace and lowers his head as though it pained him to say his next words. "Well, what is it? I mean only a moment ago I was willing to throw myself to you—you—a stranger! Only to be told you didn't want me."

"I never said I didn't want you," Lux snaps back with a low snarl. His eyes flash in what I can only make out to be frustration or anger. My footing falters slightly as I buckle at the grisly sound of his tone and my heart flutters with what should be fear. But it's not. Something about the grumbling roar rippling through Lux's chest shot straight to my femininity.

Never have I heard a sexier sound. My newly appointed passionate pixie screams *do it again* in my mind.

*Hold steady, Winter,* I inwardly scold myself.

"Please, I'm sorry, I'm working harder than you know to control myself, beautiful." Lux's husky, tone matches the warring I see behind his eyes, melting more iciness encasing me.

"Then what is it, Lux?" I whisper back, taking a few steps closer, stopping short of pulling him in my arms. "I mean are you married? Girlfriend?"

A broad smile blushes over his face and the frustration I saw brewing within him, slowly fades as he belts a slight chuckle. Amused, he grins back at me and shakes his head. "No wife. No girlfriend."

"Oh," I say on a gasp as it becomes evident the real reason for his trepidation. "I see. So it's because I'm human right? I suppose supernaturals don't usually mix with mere mortals like me."

"Mere? Oh my dear, Winter, if you only knew just how *un-mere* you truly are," Lux says as he takes another step closer.

"So you just don't like me like that then? Not into virgins? What?" I blurt, hating my retort just as soon as the words roll off my tongue.

Laughing again, Lux takes another step, fully closing the gap between us. Gently taking my face in his warm palm, he leans his head into mine. Taking a deep breath as though he were trying to inhale the essence of me wholly, he rests his thumb along the curve of my lip and smiles.

"Believe me when I say, you're the only virgin I'm interested in getting into right now. That I promise you," he breathes his words at my ear. Looking back at me, his eyes glimmer with gold and his heavy breathing tells me he's working just as hard as he said.

*Chapter Nine*

"I'm sorry, Lux, I shouldn't have come on so strong. It's not how my mother raised me I promise."

Smiling, he kisses my forehead and pulls me back into his embrace. "No worries, sweetness, I have no doubt Lady Elysian raised you with nothing but the highest standards," he adds with another chuckle.

Gripping his broad shoulders, I pull back slightly so that I can get a full view of his face. "So that was it? You want to take the lead?" I say, twirling my fingers through the plastic buttons straining to contain the breadth of him.

The way he's looking at me right now has my passionate pixie twirling with excitement.

"Well, yes and no," he answers softly. My brows scrunch at his reply, but he firms his hold on me, ensuring I'll not get away as I had before. "Yes, I want to take the lead, but not because I thought you were out of place or not being ladylike. And no I don't want us to take that big step just yet."

And just like that, my little pixie pouts, balling herself in knots. I can't help wondering how a man like Lux could want someone like me. Sensing my angst, Lux tightens his grip at my back, pushing our bodies back together.

"Do you feel that, beautiful?" Lux adds with a slight push of his hips forward. Another whimper escapes from me as he does and all manner of passion rushes to my sweet spot. "That's what you do to me. It's taking everything in me not to delight myself in the pleasure of your sweetness right now. You have no idea how hard I'm trying not to throw your cousin off that bed, imprint my wolf on you and claim every inch of you."

"Why don't you?" I mumble almost incoherently as Lux presses his manhood hard against me. He's not the only one working hard to restrain themselves.

"Because you deserve better," he says with muted breath, slowly pulling his hips away from me. "We both do."

"You're right," I swallow my resolve. "A romp in a lumberyard is hardly romantic."

"Hardly," he smiles back with a wink. "Besides, despite popular opinion, I am not a man who believes a woman's virginity is something to be conquered or taken at a whim."

Once more I push the hard air down my throat. If I didn't hear him say it myself, I'd find it hard to believe such a stallion as Luxor Decanter could say such things.

"Oh?" The shock in my tone is hard to miss.

"Especially not a woman as beautiful, strong, and wonderful as you, my dear Winter. A woman like you requires exploration. While the perfectness of your body calls to me in ways I've never experienced until now, I want to explore

*Chapter Nine*

every part of you—your mind, your soul, and your body. I want to share in life's adventures with you. I want to experience life at your side. But more than that I want to see you live your life."

The care of his words confounds me. Even through Kharon's endearing attempts, never have such words been spoken to me of him or any man. Until now. "You want that with me?" I whisper bashfully.

"Yes, beloved," Lux adds as he lifts my chin so that our eyes meet. "I want that for us. As much as I regret that I am not a virgin, I can tell you this, sex without intimacy is hollow. Just two clunky bodies looking to fulfill their carnal needs, only to learn at the end they are left unfulfilled. Believe me when I say when we make love, I want you fulfilled in every way imaginable. Every. Single. Way."

"I want that too," I breathe back.

"Good," Lux replies with a darkened glare. "I plan on filling you with all of me."

"And imprinting on me?" I question, trailing my hands along his bulking biceps.

"Ah yes, that," he smirks.

"So are you going to explain what that means exactly? What am I signing up for?" I tease.

"Oh you're signing up for all of me, my dear Winter. You're signing up to become my wife."

*One Winters Kiss*

My mouth parts in a gasp at his admission, causing the butterflies to flutter once more within me. When I woke up this morning, the name Luxor Decanter was never upon my lips. Yet with one kiss, I now know I'll utter his name every morning from this day forward.

# Chapter Ten

*Lux*

Winter has no idea how hard she is making this for me. With the way her luscious lips drape open in this moment she literally controls the strength of me. Still, my wolf is raging within me, begging me to set him free and have his way.

But I've tamed him this long and he'll just have to wait a little longer.

"Did my words frighten you?" I ask as I sense apprehension building with her.

"Well—um—I'm not frightened. A little taken aback, but not afraid." Although I can tell this is all puzzling for her, I am impressed with her resolution to hear me out.

"Good," I say as I walk her to the small wooden table near the water bar. Grabbing two bottles of water from the small fridge, I hand her one. She mumbles a quick word of thanks before hurriedly guzzling down the bottle in almost one gulp.

"So, what's this you were saying about me becoming your wife? You do realize we just met right?" She laughs, muttering under her breath, *"I know this is crazy, Winter but just go with it."*

I'm not sure if she realizes I can hear her. This is probably the second or third time I've heard her do that today. Obviously, she's unaware her private thoughts are quite audible. Or perhaps she knows and doesn't care. Either way, it's actually rather adorable.

"You were saying—" Winter blurts, gesturing for me to explain further.

"Well now I see why you need that school after all. It's quite clear either the human faction of the Regency doesn't know everything they should about supernaturals, or don't care enough to educate you."

"My point exactly," she mocks, hunching her shoulders with a quaint laugh that brightens her face. Her teasing doesn't bother me, instead I'm happy my talk of marriage isn't scaring her off.

"I'll get straight to the point. Wolves can only mate with humans to whom they are bonded by marriage. Only that sacred covenant has the

## Chapter Ten

power to bind the two as one. Even then, a human has to be strong enough to endure the mating. If not, the results can be rather dire."

"Do you mean like have enough stamina?"

"Not quite, beautiful," I cover my laugh. "I mean I suppose stamina may have something to do with it, but the wolf must also be sated. My wolf and I must be in full agreement. A wolf's senses are more keen than even an Altrinion or me in my more human-like state. If my wolf senses anything amiss he can reject the mating."

"Oh, wow!" Winter adds with another gulp as she keeps her gaze fixed on me.

"Wow indeed."

"So, does the wolf do that if you mate with other wolves?"

"No, if the wolf rejects an equal, then the matter only results in mere sex. Not a binding covenant. That's why I want—no, need you to be my wife. When we make love for the first time, we will be in agreement in every manner bound to this earth."

"Every manner?" Her words are almost inaudible but still manage to leap straight to my heart.

"Yes, beloved, every manner. How does that make you feel?" I ask, everything in me wishes to jump over this table and take her in my arms. If for no other reason than to ease her angst, it's taking everything I've got not to leap out of my seat.

Winter lifts the water bottle to her mouth once more, relishing the last sip. Her pouty lips grip the bottle almost greedily as her eyes close as if that last drop satiated every part of her being.

I've never been more jealous of a piece of plastic than I am right now.

Her lingering hold on the bottle slightly irritates me, if for no other reason than I need to know how she feels. How my words make her feel. I'm up and in front of her in a blink, startling her as I gently remove the bottle from her hand, tossing it to the ground.

"Winter," I begin, taking her hands to lift her from the chair. "I need to know how that makes you feel. Does that four-letter word scare you?"

"You mean wife?" She asks, her brow raised.

"Yes." My answer is quick as my wolf continues raging within me.

"Well, yes and no," she says as her eyes flit over my shoulder at the sound of a small cough coming from Ross's bedside.

"Please explain, Winter. I don't want to scare you. And for as much as I want us to work, I'll understand if this is all too much and too soon for you."

Slowly pulling her hands from my grip, Winter backs away from me and circles the length of the table.

## Chapter Ten

"No, you're not going too fast, Lux. As strange as it may seem you're just my speed. All I've ever wanted was someone who took one look at me and knew in that moment that I was his forever. I want the fairytale." Winter's bright eyes look back at me with such endearing hope, I know I'll do whatever I must to be worthy of the trust she's placing in me—someone she's only just met.

"Then, my beloved, you shall have whatever fairytale your heart desires. I'll make it my life's pursuit to see to your happiness daily." My tone is resolute and as she watches me, I know my words are more assuring than even I understand.

"I'm glad to hear you say that, Lux. The word wife scares me only because you're not the only one who's expressed such a notion to me today."

Shock. Awe. Rage. Those are the only words fit to describe the newly placed warring in my heart right now. "What?" I belt a low snarl.

"Please, Lux now it's my turn to explain," she starts with her hands raised with caution.

"So there *is* someone else? Who is he? Where is he?"

"No! There is no one else for me. *Except you.*" Winter's eyes plead with me as does the sweet surrender laced in her latter words.

"I'm listening," I grit through my teeth, working hard not to search the entirety of the estate looking for anyone who dares to come between me and the lovely creature staring back at me.

"His name is Kharon Nyx. He is a business associate of my father and is the wealthiest man at the shipyard. He owns the ferry fleet, *The Erebus*. It's the only one harbored on the island year-long. Most of the women think he's a catch, but I've never seen him that way. But my father—ever since I turned twenty-one, my father has tried to make us a pair."

"So he's not your boyfriend?" My words come out sharper than I intend, but I need answers. Now.

"Kharon? Please! Of course not!" Exasperation fills her face as though she were insulted that I'd suggest such a notion. "No Kharon is just someone my father fancies as my suitor! But nothing about Kharon suits me.

"So your father wants to fix you up with an older guy I suppose?"

"Well he's not my father's age, or anything," she adds while making her way back toward me. "But he's still a bit on the young side. I think I prefer someone knocking on at least a third century's door—yeah, that's more my speed," Winter says with a sly smile.

Despite my growing irritation at the thought of another man with her, I find it cute how she manages to lessen the tension building in the

*Chapter Ten*

small space we share. I'm sure even Cedric would say a woman not bothered by my broodiness is well worth her weight in gold.

A small smile creeps along my tightened jawline as she closes the gap between us. The joyful peace I feel in her presence is like none other.

This time it's her wrapping her arms around my waist, pulling our bodies back together. Although my inclination to rage about the estate remains, I find the comfort of her hold more than satisfying. And with the way her hopeful eyes search mine through her thick lashes, I can't help surrendering to her.

With Winter in my grip, I sit back in the chair with her in my lap, wrapping her legs over my waist. She wiggles a bit and seems more than pleased my manhood responds instantly to her motion. No doubt she's testing my resolve, but with the scent of her pheromones filling the air it equally pleases me to know her affection for me remains.

Still, it doesn't change the fact, I have competition. Even if it that competition only remains in the sight of her father alone. I've never thought of winning the approval of a human until now. But if it is what I must do to make Winter mine, then so be it.

"Now tell me about Mr. Kharon Nyx."

# Chapter Eleven

## *Winter*

I should've known from our first kiss Lux had no intention of letting me go. Our kiss was what I always imagined a first kiss would be. Gentle. Soft. Sweet. How a kiss with a should-be stranger could feel like home, I'll never understand. But in this instance comprehension is not a necessity.

I know how he makes me feel. And I want to feel like this forever.

That is why the discussion of Kharon cannot be put off any longer.

Lux deserves all of me. He deserves the truth.

"Again, let me assure you I do not, nor have I ever had any ounce of affection for Kharon. Ever."

Pausing, I watch the tension between Lux's brows relax as his lips curve into the sexy smile that has all my lady parts spinning in knots.

"That's good to know," he says with a squeeze of my backside as he slightly thrusts his hips forward, allowing me to feel the strength of him through the seat of my pants. Lust dances in his eyes as he pants while crushing his mouth to mine once more. "Your affection now and always belongs right here, my beautiful one," he adds with a few pecks along my jaw and neck.

"Right here," I moan back, desperately trying to contain a modicum of decency.

"Yes, right here. Consider this your throne. You'll rule and reign the entirety of me Winter Elysian. You already do," he groans at the nape of my neck.

"My throne, huh?" I answer, wrapping my arms around his neck. His eyes dart to my cleavage in his view as I firm myself deeper in his lap, enjoying the steel strength of him against my sweet spot.

"I guess I'll have to get you a crown, huh?" Lux teases with a dashing lick of his bottom lip. I nod in agreement and laugh, thankful for whatever this is happening between us right now. "But I'll have to warn you, sweetness, a crown and my ring are all you wear the next time you sit on your throne. You won't need anything else. That I promise you."

*Chapter Eleven*

"Oh?" I question, gliding my hand along his sculpted chest. "I thought I was going to remain a virgin?"

"Only until I make you my wife. Afterwards, my queen, you'll spend your days and nights seated on your throne. How does that sound?"

"Like I want to be your wife right now," I whisper, breathless. The acrobatics my lady parts are doing right now have my insides gushing with anticipation.

"Good we are certainly in agreement. But we gotta slow this down a bit. If not, I don't know if I'll be able to contain myself much longer. It's taking all my strength not to take you right now."

"Why don't you?"

"Because as I've said before, *we deserve better*. Our first time will rival the fairytales of legend and our love will endure because we had the patience to do it right from the start. Not to mention there's still the matter of Kharon Nyx and me gaining the approval of Lord Elysian. Your father is an honorable man, and he deserves my respect. More than that, I also respect you too much to treat you as some idle passion. You are it for me, Winter. Do you understand me? It. For. Me."

Lux's hold on me is steady as his hands remain firm on my butt and his manhood a fixture at my crotch. The gleam in his eyes is both hopeful and pleading as his longing stare deepens into my own. The want of me in his eyes is not lost on me either. I have no doubt if he weren't the gentleman he is, he'd strip me bare and boar his way into me.

And he'd do so with no protest from me.

But he is right, this is the fairytale I've always wanted, so I need to see it through.

"So what are we going to do about Kharon and my father?" I ask, curious as to his plan.

"Well, I suppose I need to do a little digging into who this Kharon Nyx is so that I understand who I'm dealing with. From there, I can deal with your father."

The thought of both Kharon and the matter of my father, dry up my passion well and I slowly pull myself from Lux's lap. I find it difficult to remain passionate while discussing either of them.

"Talk about a mood killer," I grumble, turning my back to clasp my shirt together. Although I find it strange, I hadn't really noticed just how much my boobs were punching their way through the linen fabric of my blouse.

"I'm sorry, beloved. But it is a conversation we must have. Don't fret, I'll simply explain to Lord Elysian that we're in love. You said he and your mother had a whirlwind romance, right? So maybe he'll understand. There's hope," Lux answers as he comes to my side and lifts my chin to meet his caring gaze.

*Chapter Eleven*

"Win," I hear Ross whine from the next room.

"Look, Winter, you should tend to your cousin. I'll see you at the festivities tonight." Planting a small kiss on my forehead, Lux pulls me in for a quick hug and makes his way to the door.

"Lux!" I shout his name over the faint whining of Ross's voice. Lux turns quickly and smiles tenderly back at me.

"Yes," he replies sweetly.

"Don't you want my number or something? I mean how will I contact you?"

"Good point. Although you should know as a wolf, I am an excellent tracker. Your scent, my lady, is forever engrained in the fabric of my mind. I'll be able to find you no matter where you are. And since I have no plans of being apart from you longer than the duration it takes until I see you tonight, getting your number didn't quite come to mind. But since I left for a run, I didn't bring my phone with me. Text me at this number, and I'll reply once I get back to my suite," Lux says while writing his number on my palm with a sharpie he grabs from the side table near the door. "This won't be the last imprint I make on you either. Think of it as a first of many," he adds with a sexy smirk and wink.

"What?" I mutter, surprised. While I have no idea what an imprint is, I have no doubt it's intimate in nature. Even more, I look forward to discovering what it means entirely.

Lux replies with a quick peck on my forehead before making his way out of the cabin. Watching him leave aches my heart, but the anticipation of knowing I'll see him later fuels me with a giddy feeling I've never known until now.

"Win?" I hear Ross's groggy voice call to me from behind.

Taking a deep breath as I close the door, I force my yearning for Lux aside, only so I can give my cousin the attention he needs. As I turn around, I smile when I see Ross's thin outline frame the doorway.

"Hey Ross, I'm sorry I've taken too long to get back to you. How are you feeling?" I ask as I make my way toward him.

"Like a bear beat me up," Ross replies, rubbing his forehead. "Yet, I feel strangely wonderful. Odd right?"

"Oh there have been quite a few odd and strange happenings today," I mutter while taking his hand to lead him to the sofa.

"You mean like you cozying up to that gargantuan wolf man like a little strumpet?" Ross says as he crosses his legs and falling deep into the corner of the sofa with his brow raised. "Well come on then, spill it missy!" He waves at me, patting the cushion next to him, gesturing me to sit next to him.

"A strumpet, eh? Really Ross?" I shake my head, laughing.

*Chapter Eleven*

Looking me up and down, Ross laughs, tossing his head back before regarding me with his all-knowing cagey grin. "Well what do you call straddling the lap of a man you've just met and pledging your—um—everything to him?"

"Everything I've ever wanted," I whisper back as memories of me in Lux's arms stir like fluttering butterflies within me. "And more," I add, looking into Ross's wide eyes.

"Woah honey! You really got bit by that love bug!" Ross stares at me with one arm folded and the other rested on his chin, sizing me up. "I have never seen you like this. I mean you're not quite a prude as auntie, but goodness knows you're her spitting image and you're normally just as stiff as she is."

"Well, yeah, but even she fell head over heels for my father when she first met him. I know my mother must understand how this feels." My words sound like more of a question than a statement, but Ross gets my point. "Right?"

"Let's hope so lovebug. Let's hope so!" Ross quietly replies as he pulls me into his shoulder.

# Chapter Twelve

*Lux*

This has to be the dumbest thing I've ever done. But for Winter, it's all worth it.

Reason tells me to go back to my suite, and get myself together before I make my case to Lord Elysian. However, my heart won't listen to reason. All it sees is opportunity.

Spotting Winter's father in the courtyard as I made my way back to my suite, I know I should commit myself to a more proper path. Yet, with him only a stone's throw from me now, I have to plead the case of my heart. If for no other reason than to elude his plan of forcing her hand in marriage to someone she does not love, I know it's now or never.

"Lord Elysian," I call to him, hoping he doesn't pick up on the nervous quiver in my tone. He turns slower on his heel than I anticipate as my anxious speed sputters me in front of him before he can reply.

"Yes?" He raises his brow in question, looking me over, likely offput by my attire.

"I know it's been a while since we last met. My name is Lux Decanter, sir. It's been more than a decade since you opened your estate. My brother, Cedric and I met you and your late son Melchior." Offering my hand toward him, he regards me warily with his cigarette hanging loosely beneath his thick mustache. "I am with the Guardians of Lord Marchand, sir," I add knowing it's likely only our leader, Dalcour Marchand's name, that is most memorable. Everyone just loves the Altrinion-Vampires.

"Ah yes," he begins, working hard to curve his mouth into a smile. "The Guardians—right—right—you're on the wolf guard. Now I remember," Lord Elysian finishes, brandishing a smile that finally meets his eyes. "Well, it's good to see you again young man," he says with less hesitance.

"Yes, sir," I acquiesce despite the fact I have him by almost three centuries. Luckily for me I've worn the face of a thirty-year old for quite some time.

"Well, it was good seeing you again, but I must get going. I'm sure I'll see you tonight at the

## Chapter Twelve

cotillion," he continues, using his cane to turn away from me to make his way inside a small brick building adjacent to the manor. Noticing his engraved name on an iron post above the large walnut door, I assume this is his office.

"If you would but allow me a moment, sir, I'd like—"

Blowing out a deep sigh, Lord Elysian shakes his head in frustration as he crosses the threshold of the door into his office. He only makes his way inside just beyond the doorpost before turning around with a tight grip on the door, preparing to close it in my face. "I'm so sorry, my boy. I really don't have time to talk right now. There's still so much for me to do in preparation for this evening. And I have a meeting with Lord Marchand and one of his associates. I am sure you can understand." His hurried tone leaves little room for interruption, but I know it's now or never.

"I need to talk to you about Winter, my lord," I force my words through the crack of the door, desperation flooding my soul.

The sharp lift of his thick, black brows tells of both his protectiveness and worry as he regards me. His posture stiffens and the once elderly and frail man who seemed dependent on his cane, stands upright before me with his defenses as high as the bear did with Winter and Ross this morning.

"Winter?" he questions, opening the door wide. "Is she okay? Did something happen?" Concern fills the void between his brows and I hear the pacing of his heart increase.

"No, my lord. It's nothing like that at all, I assure you," I begin, lifting my palms in caution. "I'm sorry I did not mean to upset you." I want to say more, but a faint, stench akin to death flares my nostrils in warning, forcing me to stop short of my reason for talking with Lord Elysian.

Looking around, I don't see anyone other than humans roaming about the grounds. Still, the repulsive smell lingers and a new warning within me grows.

"Well, then, how do you know my Win? What is this about?" Lord Elysian snaps back, bringing me back to the moment. His tone is sharper than I recall of him in years past. *Almost too sharp.* If he were any other mortal, I'd break him in two for the tenor of his voice alone, but thankfully for him, he is Winter's father. His saving grace.

Straightening my posture, trying to resume my plea, I work hard to maintain my cool so that I can help her father understand how I feel about his daughter.

"The truth is I met your daughter earlier today and she and I well, we—"

"You what?" He says narrowing his gaze and using his cane to lean into me across the threshold.

## Chapter Twelve

Stepping back, I offer a smile, but it does little to assuage his gnawing angst. "Well sir, Winter and I really hit it off and got to know one another."

"Is that so? I doubt you got to know anything about my daughter. My Win doesn't just go about her days *hitting it off* with fellows—especially not fellows like yourself."

Holding back my wolf's inclination to tear into him, I work to quiet my wolf's raging, while holding my ground. "Ah yes, that may be sir, Winter actually told me quite a bit about herself. You know, like the school she wants to start here and—"

"School? What school? You know nothing about my daughter! Win knows her obligation to Elysian Manor and has endeavored herself to take charge of the business of things here. But you already knew that didn't you?"

"What? No!" I protest, stepping back as I sense Elysian's anger closing the gap between us.

"Look young man—wolf—or whatever you are, I know your kind. Others in the Regency have long known of desolate wolves such as yourselves. On the verge of becoming packless Skull wolves, you lure any unsuspecting wealthy mortal to your cause for no other reason than to propagate your bloodline! And by the looks of you that is most surely your intent! I'll not have the likes of you pawn your way into my precious daughter's life and certainly not her bed!"

"Lord Elysian! I would never do that! I have no need to do such things. You do not understand, I am a hy—"

"You are a low life wolf seeking to claw your way into my daughter's life and I will not have it! My Win will never—"

"But sir, you don't understand, I love—"

"How dare you?"

"What's going on here?" A raspy voice from behind Lord Elysian interrupts our forming stand-off.

"Kharon! Thank God for you! Would you please send this lone wolf packing! I want him off my property!"

Just as Kharon's name flows from Lord Elysian's lips, a deep growl churns through me. Looking at the tall, dark blonde man with piercing gray eyes now standing behind Winter's father staring back at me sends both mine and my wolf's fury into overdrive. Even my wolf hates him.

Everything in me wants to make imperfect his perfect jawline and tear through his muscular frame outlined beneath his fit blue shirt and black trousers. Looking at the copper scorpion emblem hanging around his thick neck my mind calculates how fast I can choke him with it and possibly knock out the pearly white teeth now beaming at Winter's father with comfort.

*Chapter Twelve*

I don't care how wonderful Elysian may think Kharon Nyx may be for Winter. He is not and never will be the man for her.

I am that man.

"Why don't we all calm down," Kharon begins with a broad, luminous smile as he pats Lord Elysian's shoulder in consolation. Elysian grabs Kharon's hand in return, thankful for the gesture, granting him a small smile before returning his scowl back toward me. "Now what's going on?"

"I'll tell you what's going on, I was having a private conversation with Lord Elysian," I grit through my teeth. My wolf tenses inside as the rank odor emitting from Kharon sends my senses into a frenzy.

Kharon darts a sharp glance over Elysian's shoulder at me but softens his gaze as he looks back at him. "No need to get hasty, friend. Now I thought I heard someone mention Win?"

*"Her name is Winter!"* I bark as both men step back when I see the golden flash of my eyes mirrored in their own.

"How dare you!" Lord Elysian charges at me, using his cane as leverage. Even as he makes his way toward me, my attention is kept on Kharon Nyx. Snarling, my nostrils flare as I detect the same rank aroma now coming from Kharon, sending my supernatural senses into overdrive.

Something about him disturbs me.

Kharon pulls Lord Elysian back before he ever crosses the threshold, but Winter's father uses his cane to jab my shoulder, threatening me with some curses that fly right over my head. My focus remains on Kharon. His scent isn't mortal. But it isn't familiar. Whatever it is, it can't be good.

"Kharon, I don't care what you have to do—get this beast off my property!" Elysian shouts.

*"Beast?"* My growl resounds louder than I intend, but there's no way I'll tolerate such insults. Even if this man is to one day be my in-law.

"My word! What did I stumble upon?" I hear a heavy and familiar voice announce from behind me.

"Well, it's about time you arrived, Lord Marchand!" Elysian says, almost exasperated as he pulls himself from Kharon's hold, pushing his way past me.

It takes all my will power and affection for Winter not to throw her father clear across the island, but I remind myself that this is just a misunderstanding.

"Will you please do something about this straggly wolf you've got loose on my property?"

"Oh I assure you, Lord Elysian whatever your concerns, young Lux here can be more than amicable. Isn't that right Cedric?" Turning to see Cedric now at Dalcour Marchand's side fills me with both dread and peace.

## Chapter Twelve

Dread because the expression on his face tells me he's completely embarrassed by me. Peace because with the way I feel right now, I know only my brother can rein my inhibitions.

"Why of course, my lords. I am certain Lux meant no offense," Cedric offers with a placating smile and daggered eyed gaze at me to match.

"Well, Lord Marchand all I ask is that you keep him and his mangy paws away from my precious daughter, Win!"

"Her name is Winter!" I roar back. I've grown tired of trying to be Mr. Nice Guy.

"Do you see his insolence? He dares correct her own father. In his presence and on his property? Surely this is not the manner of your Guard?" Kharon says now coming to Elysian's side. Another roar rumbles through my chest and Cedric quickly makes his way beside me, firming a tight hold on my shoulder. His eyes quickly dart to Kharon and his lips curl as he observes him. Even Cedric knows something is off. "I mean, I am her fiancé and even I have never spoken in such a manner!" Kharon yells back.

"You are not her fiancé! But if you get close to Winter ever again, I'll snatch the remnants of your hollowed soul through the maggot hole in your gut!" I growl, flexing my posture and preparing to shift. Cedric wraps his arms around me, forcing me to calm myself as he uses the full weight of his strength to keep me from phasing and ripping Kharon's head from his body.

"Lux!" Dalcour shouts my name as he makes his way in front of me and blocking my view of both Kharon and Elysian as Cedric keeps a tight hold on me from behind. My canines lengthen and I feel my muscles protruding beneath my tightly borrowed lumber attire. "Take hold of yourself! Now! That's an order!" The flash of crimson in Dalcour's Altrinion-Vampire eyes lets me know I'm threatening even his resolve.

"Get him out of my sight!" Lord Elysian commands, pointing his cane at me with anger marring his face.

Neither Cedric nor Dalcour wastes time removing me from his presence as they use their vampiric speed to carry me in flight and away from Winter's father. Although this wasn't the way I intended to make my intentions known to her father, I now know my challenge far outweighs some would-be suitor or her father's approval.

My real problem is uncovering the truth behind Kharon Nyx.

# Chapter Thirteen

## *Winter*

Walking back to the manor, Ross is more silent now than I've ever known of him as he listens to me recount my time with Lux. In all our years, I know he's never seen me carry on about a man this way. Ever.

Usually it's me and Rae who sit and listen to Ross's many escapades. While I've never thought much about any man on this island, Rae has only shared interest in a few; most notably Kharon Nyx. Maybe if my father hadn't turned Kharon's attention toward me years ago, Rae would have a better chance.

*One Winters Kiss*

In all fairness, I really wish she went after him. But being the dutiful and sweet cousin she is, she'd never do anything like that.

"So let me get this straight," Ross says, grabbing my wrist tight, stopping us at the base of the stairs to the house. "You want to marry this guy? But you only spent a few hours with him."

"Well, I mean he didn't propose or anything but—"

"Look cousin, you know I love you but you gotta admit this is moving a little fast don't you think? Shouldn't you two be getting to know each other better first?" Ross's quiet tone is void of his usual sass. He's serious.

"Okay and if you know me Ross, you know I've never experienced anything like this before. You know I'm not going to let anyone rope me into just anything. I've waited for what seems like forever for someone—no, *the one*—to come in and sweep me off my feet. Now, for the first time in my life, I finally feel like I've found it. No, I have found him."

Ross's deep gaze burrows into the depths of my eyes as he searches my face. I can't tell if it's the winter's chill bringing out the red in his toffee-coated cheeks or what I just said, but I know for sure he heard me. A small smile pierces through his bleak expression and his hold on me lessens.

"You're right, Win. I have never seen you like this before. And you're right, you're way too stubborn to let someone just finagle their way into your heart. So whatever this is you're feeling baby girl, go for it! I'm behind you one thousand percent. But know this, if he turns out to be a dud, I promise you I'll have Stephen and the whole lumber squad on his ass in a heartbeat! Yep, I said it! On his ass!"

Throwing his lanky arms around me, we both laugh as Ross pulls me in for a hug. Our laughter continues as we make our way up the stairs. Even though I'm older than Ross and Rae by two years, Ross has always acted like an older brother, threatening anyone he thinks mean either me or Rae harm. While I have every hope to believe Lux has nothing to fear from Ross, I know my cousin would indeed go the distance for me if he thought it necessary.

"Well, since you mentioned Stephen," I begin with a chuckle as Ross holds the door open for me. "You never did tell me what happened in the pine fields last night."

"Oh honey, there's so much to tell. First we—"

"Where have you two been?" Rae shouts as she rounds the corner into the foyer as Ross closes the door behind us. "Uncle El and Auntie have been looking for you, Win! And they don't seem happy."

Ross looks at me and laughs, patting my back and I bashfully smile knowing he's eager to spill the goods on my time with Lux to Rae. The twins don't keep secrets from one another and that includes even my secrets.

"All right cousin, I guess you better drip that tea—before I do, honey!" Ross giggles.

"I don't know what tea you two have going on, but I can tell you Uncle El's tea is piping hot! Now where have you been?" Rae forces her words through her teeth as her eyes dance up toward the staircase where I hear the loud grumbling sound of my father from a distance.

"Hold on, Rae, what's going on?" I ask over Ross's continued laughter as I watch worry cloud Rae's face. It's uncommon for my usually jolly cousin to be worried about anything.

"That's what I'd like to know, young lady!" My father shouts down from the top of the stairs.

"My thoughts exactly," Mother adds. "Winter Marie Elysian, you have some explaining to do!"

Looking up at the frowns etched on both my parents' faces wrenches my insides.

"I'm sorry, uncle," Ross says coming in front of me. "I pulled Win away from Kharon to go with me to the pine fields and while we were out there, we got approached by a bear."

"A bear?" Both my mother and Rae gasp in unison.

"Yes, a bear. Well, he brushed me with a bit of a good pounding, and I hit my head. Winter and um---a friend—took me to the cabin to tend to

*Chapter Thirteen*

me. We've been there ever since. But see I'm all better now!"

"You expect me to believe you?" Father snaps back. "A bear, really? Ross barely has a scratch on him!"

'Yes, uncle it was bear. Honest!" Ross says with his hands lifted in surrender.

"And were there any other *beasts* out there with you?" Father grinds the words through his teeth as he makes his way down the stairs with Mother at his heels.

"Father?" His question confuses and troubles me. "What do you mean, any other beasts? Didn't you just hear what Ross said, a bear attacked us!" I counter, now stepping in front of Ross.

"I can only wonder why a bear attacked you. Perhaps he was more fearful of the wolf you've been entertaining!" Father yells back.

Ross and I glance at one another with parted lips, shocked.

"How do you know?" I whisper, stepping back as my parents make their way in front of me.

"So it is true? You've been with that lone wolf man all day!" Father shouts.

"Win, darling, please tell me you didn't!" Mother huffs, holding her hand at her heart.

"Ross! Rae! Please leave us!" My father demands, using his cane to point them toward the family room.

"Rae, please take Ross to the back and make sure he's okay," my mother adds as her gaze softens as she looks at Ross. However, her eyes darken when she turns her attention back to me.

"Win, I am very disappointed in you! I thought we raised you better than that!" My father begins. As he speaks, I can't help wondering how he knows. Perhaps one of the lumbermen came back to the cabin and got an eyeful of me and Lux. Maybe Kharon followed us? I don't know. All I know is whatever my father knows has him more furious than I've ever seen him.

"Disappointed in me? For what?" I need to understand just how much he knows. I may have kissed Lux, but we certainly didn't go the distance. Little does he know, he only has Lux to thank for that.

"Win, please tell us you didn't run off on the proposal of a very decent man, to do heaven knows what with this wolf fellow?" My mother says with her hands clasped tight at her waist.

"No need of asking her, Vivian, because that is exactly what she did!" Father bites back.

"That is not what I did! Look, I don't know where you're getting your information from but—"

"But nothing, young lady! I've got this information straight from the horse's mouth. As if it wasn't shock enough to learn you evaded Kharon's proposal with that phony run-off with

## Chapter Thirteen

Ross—and no, I'm not buying that bear story—but to now learn you did so to be with some wolf man!"

"Wolf man?" I snap, I don't like where this is going. "Do you mean Lux? How do you know about Lux?"

"Oh I have my ways, missy! And those ways come easy when desperate, raggedy wolves go hunting for the first unassuming mortal they can find!"

"What are you talking about? Lux didn't go hunting for me. As a matter of fact we only met because he scared off the bear and helped me take care of Ross," I protest.

"Just give it up, Win, I know there was no bear. Besides, the bears have lived peacefully near us for years without so much of an incident."

"Oh really? Then why do you tell me to always carry a pistol? Why did you teach me that learning to use a rifle was more important than ice skating lessons? Because there are bears!"

"Ah yes, and did you take your pistol?"

"Well, no but"

"But nothing, Win! Even you know this cockamamie story is just your excuse because you were out frolicking with that wolf man!"

"And you haven't told me how or what you know about Lux." I yell, matching my father's stubbornness.

"Your father knows when his daughter is too naïve and vulnerable to notice when someone is trying to take advantage of her!" Mother lashes back.

"Naïve! About what? Love?" I holler, tossing my hands behind my neck in frustration as I circle the large EM marble logo of our foyer.

"Love? What do you know about love? This is lust—plain and simple!" Father grumbles, leaning into staircase with his arms folded.

"Listen, mom, dad," I start, working hard to remain calm. "I don't know what you heard about me and Lux but let me assure you this is not some fleeting schoolgirl crush. I think—no I know—he's the one!"

"Win!" Both my parents cry out in unison, incensed.

"I know, I know it seems like a whirlwind, but believe me when I tell you, it's just like when you two fell in love. You know how you met, fell in love with one another and married in a manner of weeks." My eyes glass with tears as I speak, hopeful the memory of their courtship will bring about some understanding.

"Now you see, Vivian, why I told you to stop filling her head with those fairytales! Now look at her! I told you she deserved the truth when she was a child because now—well, you heard her!" Father sighs, rubbing his balding scalp as he walks

## Chapter Thirteen

off into his study. "Tell her Vivian!" he shouts from the distance.

"Tell me what?" I mumble, watching my mother's careful steps toward me. Her gaze has softened as I watch a heavy heart consume the entirety of her being.

"I'm sorry, Win, your father is right, I should've told you this before. I should have told you the truth." Mother's tone is eerily calm and her eyes just as glassy as my own.

"The truth about what?"

"About your father and me. We didn't have the whirlwind romance I told you."

"What?" I say in disbelief.

"His first wife, Diane, was ill and I was sent as a nurse to care for her. Melchior was away at boarding school and your father was so busy with his business. But he was lonely. We both were. As Diane's condition got worse, your father and I grew close. Very close."

"Mother! You didn't!" I gasp, as the revelation of her words paint a picture I never hoped to see.

"*We did.*" Remorse fills her face as she regards the steps I take away from her.

"Diane passed quietly and by that time your father and I were in love."

"So everything you told me was a lie? It was all a lie!" I shout, watching my usually staunch mother quiver at my words.

"I'm sorry, darling," she cries. Wiping her tears with her wrists, she closes the space between us and continues. "But your father is right, I painted a fairytale in your mind and now you think this lone wolf is coming like a knight in shining armor to sweep you off your feet. Well, I'm so sorry, dear, but that's just storybook talk. That isn't how the world works."

Brushing my own tears aside and choking down the knot in my throat, I take a deep breath. "Well, Mother it may not be how the world works or you and father for that matter. But this is my heart—my world—and Lux will be a part of it, whether you and father like it or not."

## Chapter Fourteen

*Lux*

"Have you lost your mind!" Cedric shouts, tossing me into the sofa like a ragdoll. "What in the world has gotten into you?" Jumping back up to meet my brother's darted stare, a loud growl erupts through me, causing a trembling force to shake throughout our suite.

"Hey! What's the matter you two?" I hear Abigail call coming from the bedroom.

"Why don't you ask your brother-in-law? He's the one picking fights with the Regency leaders!" Cedric yells back.

"I am not the one picking fights, brother, but I have every intention on finishing one!"

"Lux, stop it! You too Cedric!" Lord Marchand orders, now coming in between me and Cedric. With his hands raised at our chests, his crimson eyes flash with warning to both of us. Grunting, we back away from one another, yet neither of us is committed to surrender.

"Now will someone explain what is going on here?" Abigail says, rounding the corner of the couch. I notice she's still sipping blood from her tumbler as she was earlier. With the cotillion only hours away, I know my sister-in-law is doing her best to manage her bloodlust. Rehabilitated or not, Scourge Vampires are always thirsty.

"Abigail is right," Dalcour begins. "I think we deserve some explanation."

"What is there to explain, my lord? My brother hates humans! You saw as much earlier. He'd rather pick a fight with them than stand in civility along side them. And it was my mistake for bringing him here!"

If this were yesterday, I would agree with my brother wholeheartedly. But one chance encounter with Winter Elysian has changed me in ways that are inexplicable. From the first time I saw her, I wanted to protect her, love her, and explore the entirety of my existence with her. Lust is a feeling I'm well accustomed to. This wasn't lust. This was love. *It is love.* She totally enraptured me and has my head spinning so fast I can barely think.

*Chapter Fourteen*

"I mean, look at him, my lord! He sits there staring off into space with nothing to say for himself!" Cedric blows out an air of frustration as his arms lay folded at his chest while he paces around the suite.

"Is this true, Lux? Does being around the humans bother you too much?" Dalcour questions, while seating himself on a small chair opposite me.

I want to respond to him but I'm working hard to keep Kharon's scent in the forefront of my mind. Something about him feels off. As irritated as I may be at Winter's father, at least I know his only concern is for his daughter. Kharon is another matter entirely.

"Do you see what I mean, Lord Marchand? All you'll get from this one is apathy. When it comes to the humans, he cares nothing for the cause of civility you wish to maintain. He doesn't even care to understand the very reason you travel the globe having these cotillions is to bring about harmony between the supernatural and mortal worlds. I had hoped after all these years he would at least have a sense of propriety about such things, but alas—"

"Are you finished, Cedric!" I holler, slowly rising from my seat. "If you would just listen for a moment, you might learn after I left you this morning, I ran into a human girl—no, a woman— who has my mind turning about in ways I never knew possible. So no, I may have never cared much for humans before, but now—now I think I love one."

There, I said it. As much as I never thought I'd ever profess the word, I've done the impossible. And I'd gladly say it again. *I love Winter Elysian.*

Looking around the suite, every mouth is parted in surprise. Both Abigail and Dalcour's faces mirror the happiness I feel inside. Cedric, on the other hand, looks as though he sees a ghost.

"Lux, this is wonderful news!" Abigail squeals, using her vampiric speed to be at my side in an instant, throwing her arms around my waist. Squeezing tight, she kisses my cheek and I grimace, rolling my eyes. It isn't enough she's overly affectionate with my brother, now it's spilling over to me. "Isn't it, dearest!"

With her hand still locked tight, Abigail rests her head on my shoulder and smiles at Cedric. His eyes are still laden in shock but I see his posture soften. Cedric, more than anyone, knows how I feel.

"Brother, are you saying what I think you're saying?" Cedric asks, leaning against the wall with his hands fisted together.

"I think your brother is saying he met his mate," Dalcour adds, leaning back into his seat with an appreciative smile that stretches the width of his face.

*Chapter Fourteen*

"Yes, I met someone," I answer, playfully shaking out from under Abigail's grip. "Her name is Winter. Winter Elysian."

"Ah, this does explain things a little," Dalcour begins. "So I take it Lord Elysian isn't too keen on his daughter being with a wolf?"

"He thinks I'm some low-level lone wolf seeking to latch onto a wealthy suitor, so as not to fall to a Skull wolf's curse. I tried to explain, but he didn't give me a chance."

"Well, why don't you leave that up to me? It's been a while since we've had dealings with this Regency. I'm sure if I explain to him that hybrids can't fall into such a curse, he'll understand. Besides, I have history with the Elysian family. I helped his great-grandmother, Greta, from almost falling into such a fate many years ago when she first came to Canada. I am sure that is why he is leery of you."

"Oh, now you see, Lux, it's just a matter of clearing things up." Cedric's face brightens as he pushes away from the wall. "If need be, I'll help Lord Marchand explain things to Winter's father."

"But there's more," I interject just as Cedric and Lord Marchand begin collaborating their strategy.

"What is it, Lux?" Abigail asks softly as she places her tumbler on the coffee table, carefully watching my grim expression cloud my face.

"Lord Elysian has already promised her hand to someone else." Deep gasps echo throughout the suite and Abigail cups her mouth with her hands.

"Was it the man with him earlier?" Cedric's eyes flash with crimson as he makes his way toward me. Shaking my head, a low hiss churns through my brother along with an expletive in Italian.

"Yes. What do you know, brother?"

"I think we all know whoever he is—he isn't mortal!" Lord Marchand says, rising from his seat.

"I knew there was something off about him!" I exclaim. "At first, I thought I was just out of sorts because of Lord Elysian's reaction to me. But his scent threw me off."

"Indeed! It threw me off as well. But I was so focused on your behavior toward Lord Elysian I shrugged it off."

"Well, since he is clearly not with us or a true member of the Regency, I think we need to look into this man further. Lux, do you know his name or anything else about him?" Dalcour asks.

"His name is Kharon Nyx. He manages the largest ferry fleet, *The Erebus*, on the island. Winter said he was wealthy. Even if he were just some mortal, I'd do whatever it took to keep him away from Winter, but since it's obvious he's

## Chapter Fourteen

something more, I worry his intentions will not only harm her, but her family."

"Lord Marchand, what do you think? Do you think this man could really be a danger?" Deep wrinkles of concern fade my sister-in-law's otherwise soft features. Cedric wraps his arm around his wife, adding a consoling kiss to the crown of her head.

"I don't know, Abigail," Lord Marchand starts, with his hand tucked under his chin. "But one thing is clear, he is neither vampire, wolf, nor any earthbound supernatural I've known to walk this earth. Not in my five hundred plus years on this Earth nor in the long years of my father before me have I ever known of a creature with his distinct scent. Whatever he is, Lux has reason to fret, if for no other reason than the safety of his beloved and her family. Even more, it may be the safety of humanity itself is at risk if we don't uncover his truth and soon."

"Then what are we waiting for? Let's go!" I shout, making my way to the door.

"Slow down, young one." Dalcour is in front of me before I have a chance to grab the doorknob. His reddened eyes and the Altrinion embers of fire upon his skin flash before me in an instant. "We can't just go throwing unfounded accusations around to Lord Elysian. Your run in with him earlier has already painted you in an unbecoming light."

Snarling growls rumble through me as I lock eyes with Dalcour. I know I should listen to reason, but all my thoughts are of Winter. Knowing her father insists on marrying her off to someone who may have less than honorable intentions mounts a protective rage I've never known until now.

"Lord Marchand is right, brother. Calm yourself. Gather your composure. Don't let your wolfen instincts get the best of you." Cedric's hand is now on my shoulder, but everything in me wants to shake it off, run out of this room, find Winter, and take her away from this place. But I know better.

"Lux, please, if you won't do it for your brother, do it for Winter." My sister-in-law's syrupy sweet tone breaks through the fuming fog clouding my judgement. "If you love her as I can see you do, then she deserves the very best of you."

At her words, my stiff stance relaxes as I turn to see both Cedric and Abigail's caring smiles looking back at me. "Well, well baby brother, I suppose now you know just how crazy love makes you feel. Welcome to the club." Looking at me as though I just climbed a mountain, pride alone swells his chest.

As chaotic as I feel inside, one thing is true. This must be love.

# Chapter Fifteen

*Winter*

"Whether we like it or not? Is this really how we raised you, Win?" The pained tone of my father's voice startles me from behind, breaking up the forming stand-off between Mother and me.

"Father, I—"

"No, Winter, let me finish. I would've never allowed these supernaturals anywhere near my family or this estate if I'd known this would be the outcome. But when Lord Marchand saved your great-great grandmother from being taken by a pack of savage wolves long ago, our family became bound to this fate."

"I don't understand," I say, turning to see my father resting into his favorite window seat with a weathered looking scroll bound with a leather strip held across his lap.

"During slavery, many escaped to Canada as did your great-great grandparents. But their story was a little different. Your great-great grandmother, Greta, was actually rescued from slavery in Louisiana by Lord Dalcour Marchand, the leader of supernatural regency. He brought her and a few others to the Canadian border, giving her enough money to start life here in Nova Scotia. At the time your great-great grandfather, Austin, had not yet left his employ with Marchand back in Louisiana so Greta came here alone. That's when a rogue wolf, Simeon, took notice of her. Every chance he could, Simeon made advances toward Greta, but she was strong-willed and never succumbed to him. But wolves, like Simeon don't just give up. Because wolves have a need to propagate their bloodline, they'll do so at any cost. Anything to avoid falling to their fate of a Skull wolf's curse."

"A what? Father, you aren't making any sense."

"Just hear him out, Win." Mother wipes the tears from her face and straightens the would-be wrinkles in her dress. "There are just some things we should have told you long ago."

Watching the ominous expressions stretched across my parents' faces wrangles knots in my

## Chapter Fifteen

gut. Lightly placing her hand on my father's shoulder, Mother nods for him to continue.

Heaving a heavy sigh, Father begins unraveling the scroll in his hand. "When a lone wolf is found without a pack, a mate, or the wealth and resources necessary to maintain in their human-like form, they are cursed to become a Skull wolf. A savage, packless, beast. And it's that savagery I'm trying to save you from. I'll not have some lone wolf grip his claws in you because he sees your wealth and only wants you to continue his wretched bloodline!"

"I'm sorry about what happened to great-great grandmother Greta, but her story is not the same as my own! Lux is not some savage, lone wolf."

"And how would you know that, Win? You only just met him today." Mother questions, stepping closer toward me.

"Because I just know." Squeezing my eyes shut, forcing my tears aside, I know I don't sound convincing.

"If Lord Marchand hadn't arrived in time to save Greta and bring Austin along, who knows what her fate may have been. She fought tooth and nail against Simeon, holding her ground for as long as she could. But as a single woman of color being pressured into marriage with threats of being turned back over to slave catchers, her back was up against the wall. And now two hundred years later, I see the same wolf savagery threatening its way into my family. But I will not allow that wolf, Lux, or whatever his name is to try to entangle you with the likes of him!"

"No, father! No! That's not what Lux is trying to do. He cares for me—he really does!" I cry.

Opening my eyes, my father stands square before me. His eyes glassy pools of their own, he offers the scroll toward me. "Win, I am so sorry. This is not what I wanted for you. I've worked hard my whole life to provide a good life for my family. I know I should've shared the ways of the supernatural regency with you before now, but I can keep it from you no longer. Open this." Father's commanding tone is soft, but the hesitancy in his hand as he gives me the scroll, tells me this is harder for him than I can imagine.

"What is this?" I question, unraveling the scroll.

"Just one key to your legacy, I'm afraid. I should have shown this to you long before now."

Clinching the curled, worn paper in my hands, I see the words LEGEND OF REGENCY written in thick script at the top. My eyes search over the long document expanding the length of my torso, I see the words Altrinion, Vampire, Bulwarks, and Changelings headline the first half. Under each heading lists a description of each supernatural creature with associated warnings. The second half is all about wolves. Subheadings of Prime Wolves, Pack Wolves, and Dunes Wolves, have a

## Chapter Fifteen

similar layout, yet they all draw clear lines to The Curse of Skull in bold lettering below.

"Do you see it?" Father's raspy voice almost chokes his words out as he speaks. Looking up at my father through thick wet lashes, his eyes meet mine and I can see how showing this to me is no easy task. "What does it say about The Curse of the Skull? Read it out loud, Winter." Once more his demanding tone wrenches my insides in knots, but as much as it hurts me to acknowledge it, I know my father means me no pain.

Gulping the thick air in my throat, I grunt out the words before me. "By the Order of Altrinion, all earthbound will abide by the form of man. Walking this earth in his likeness and stature, wolves of lunar succession must not be found deserted, barren, or lacking earthbound affinity and mammon. Dereliction is akin to apostasy. Wolves forgone as such break the bonds of succession and kinship of MAN; forever cursed to a hollowed, soulless form. A Skull. A desolate, monstrosity."

"This can't be! This can't be!" I shriek, dropping the scroll to the floor. Memories of the first time I saw Lux, being in his arms, and our first kiss flood my mind. How could I be such a fool! I should know better.

*I know better.*

"I am so sorry, darling," Mother cries with me, pulling me into her strong embrace. "I never wanted this to happen to you!"

"The blame rests with me," Father adds, wrapping his arms around both Mother and me. "If only I had been honest with you, we could've spared you this pain."

Slowly coming out from under Father's hold, I wrap my arms around my waist, wiping the remaining tears from my chin with my free hand.

"Listen, Win," Father begins in a low tone. "This is the reason why I wanted someone like Kharon Nyx for you. Not only has he proven himself a strong, and loyal ally but he is a good man. A human. Not some opportunistic wolf looking to save himself from ruin, but a good man who wants for nothing save a family to one day call his own."

"But Father, I don't love Kharon, much less want to build a life with him!"

"I do not say these things to obligate you, sweet girl, but I do so as a father looking for someone to watch over you when I am long gone. I know, I know, he's much older than you, but while it wasn't the romantic fairytale, you thought it to be, your mother and I yet found love with one another despite our age gap."

"Your father is right, Win. To be honest, I can't say that marrying someone much older than me was high on my list when I was your age, but we made it work. Unlike my friends who struggled for years with their younger husbands, I had

## Chapter Fifteen

someone in your father who was already grounded and mature. As a result, our union was much happier than many of my friends."

Palming my face, I mute my inner screams crying for release. No sooner learning Lux's intentions were not as I'd hoped, are my parents ramming the topic of Kharon Nyx down my throat.

"I—I just can't talk about Kharon right now." My voice is a mix of a scream and a plea as tears flood my face. "I'm still trying to digest what you just shared about Lux. While the time I spent with him may have been brief, it felt real—it felt very real to me!"

"I am so sorry, darling," Mother says, coming to my side and wrapping her arm around my waist. "Your father just doesn't want you to get duped by some fast-talking wolf who only wants you so he can escape some curse. You deserve better than that. You do understand that, right?"

Parting my lips to reply, Father doesn't give me the opportunity. "Listen, Win, I will always do what I believe is in your best interest. Right now, I believe that to be Kharon. I am not saying you have to marry him tomorrow. Heck you could have a long engagement and spend a year getting to know one another. No need to rush. Just please, trust me. Because, Win, I won't be around always, but everything I do is to ensure that when that time comes, you will be all right."

"Father, I love you, but please know I'll be fine with or without Kharon. *Or any man*. You two raised me to be strong and to look after our family. I can and will always put our family first. If you want me to care for the estate and our family business, I will. But what I will not do is marry someone I do not love—not even for you." Staring back at me, my father sees his own stubbornness mirrored in my eyes. I am not backing down. Wiping my remaining tears, I turn to walk upstairs. As I do, I feel my mother's strong grip take my elbow.

"Win, we're not done. Where are you going?"

Taking in a deep breath, I force out my next words. "Well Mother, I still have a business to run, so I'm going upstairs to change. Next, I'll check in on things with the staff to ensure everything is still in order for tonight. I'll not allow my one moment's lack of judgement cause you to doubt my duty to this estate. I've worked hard to ensure tonight goes off without a hitch and I have every intention on seeing it through. So if you'll both excuse me." Turning quickly before my parents can reply, I brush one lone tear from my cheek and walk upstairs. This is the last tear I'll shed today.

# Chapter Sixteen

*Lux*

I am a nervous wreck! All my thoughts are of Winter and getting her out from under the clutches of Kharon Nyx. As much as it would pain me to do so, a part of me would even grovel at the feet of Lord Elysian until he listened to reason. Whatever pride I have I'd gladly toss aside to ensure Winter was forever in my life.

"So, tell us more about Winter," Abigail says, interrupting my thoughts. I've spent the last half hour sharing with her and Cedric about our encounter in the woods and a little about our time in the cabin. Both my brother and his wife seem genuinely interested in the first woman who has me in a tailspin.

Dalcour chimes in intermittently, popping in and out of the conversation at various points, trying to show interest. Although, while I'm sure he's happy for me, most of his concern rests with learning more about Kharon Nyx. I'm sure it doesn't sit well with him that there is some other supernatural creature roaming about under his nose. To get to the truth, he's spent the majority of his time calling Nara, the keeper of our annals and Trieu, one of his most trusted Altrinion advisors. But it was when he called his wretched and wicked brother, Decaux, for advice that I knew there was truly cause to worry. Things have to be pretty bad for him to seek out Decaux.

While I want to tell Abigail and Cedric more about Winter, I can't keep my eyes off Dalcour's continued pacing as he makes his calls. I do my best to try to eavesdrop, but my sister-in-law and brother's constant questioning isn't making it easy.

"Come on, brother, tell us more," Cedric adds, squeezing my knee. "And don't worry, Lux, Lord Marchand will share what he learns. Just keep your mind on your woman." With a quick eye wink to me as Abigail drapes her head on his shoulder, the knowing smirk etched on my brother's face tells me he's quite happy with me.

Sighing, and turning a bit so that Dalcour isn't in my direct view, I try to think of something to

## Chapter Sixteen

say that has nothing to do with the passion we shared. That is no one's business but our own. "Well, she went to school for education and is only a semester shy of completing her graduate degree. She wants to open a school for children in the Regency. You know to teach them about this supernatural world."

"Wow!" Abigail squeals. "That's rather impressive! I've never heard of such. I mean, I think it's needed, but it sounds like such a large undertaking."

"Abigail is right, Lux. Your lady does have quite lofty ambitions for a mortal. But a very admirable ambition indeed."

"Yes, Winter is a high achieving woman, that's for sure. She is also very dutiful, to a fault. When her father got ill, she took time away from school to care for the estate and the business. She is responsible for maintaining not only the manor but also planned almost every aspect of tonight's cotillion. In fact, I have no doubt Winter Elysian can do anything she puts her mind to." The pride now swelling my chest as I speak of Winter makes me happier than I've ever been.

"Well brother, that explains why you like her as you do. You've never cared much for needy, overly dependent dames," Cedric laughs.

"He's not wrong, Lux!" Abigail chuckles along with Cedric. "I remember that one girl you shagged some years ago—what was her name again?? Oh I remember, Caroline!"

"Oh yes! I remember her!" Cedric adds. "She is the reason we kept singing, *Sweet Caroline*, if I recall."

"I hate that song," I grumble, shamefully stuffing my head between my palms. "I think she called me like every hour on the hour. I got a new phone and changed my number because of her!"

"Yes, yes! She was pretty clingy for an Altrinion," Abigail continues.

"Indeed! But I blame you brother," I reply, swatting my brother's shoulder. "If you hadn't gone on about how I needed to find someone like you did Abigail, I wouldn't have given that annoying twit a second thought."

"Aww, be nice Lux, she wasn't a twit!" Abigail playfully counters, rolling her eyes up to the ceiling. "Well, maybe she was a bit dimwitted. She kept apologizing for wearing silver around me and being shocked that I had a reflection in the mirror."

"I suppose even she bought into the cinematic portrayal of vampires." Shaking his head, Cedric sighs at the thought. "But that does bring up a good point." Looking at me with one brow raised, I can almost see the calculating thoughts dancing in his mind.

"Spit it out, Cedric," I blow out, leaning back into the sofa with my arms folded across my chest.

*Chapter Sixteen*

"Well, I was just thinking about young Caroline. She was an orphaned Altrinion. But unlike us, she didn't get to benefit from the wisdom and tradition of her family."

"Yeah, so?" I hunch, wondering where my brother is going with this. I certainly don't want to dwell on Caroline much longer.

"This school you say Winter wants to start—would there be supernaturals there as well?"

At his question, I sit up, intrigued. "Interesting that you ask, brother. I actually told Winter the school should consist of more than mortal children in the Regency, but supernatural as well. After we discussed it, I think she was pretty taken with the idea."

"I mean, I'm not trying to hijack her dream or anything, but I think that would be an excellent idea. Our recent census data revealed that supernatural youth aren't living nearly as long as they should. Most barely make it past a mortal's normal lifespan. I would say lack of education is the leading cause. But what if they had a place where they could go to learn about who and what they are—"

"And how to live this life successfully," Abigail interjects, nodding in agreement.

"Wow, Lux, I don't know, but I think your lady may be onto something big." Resting his chin on his clasped fist, Cedric stares distantly across the room, mulling over the idea.

"She may be onto something bigger than even she knows," Lord Marchand adds, coming back into the living room. "I just got off the phone with everyone and what I think we just discovered about this Kharon Nyx is more than I imagined."

Quickly rising to my feet, I table thoughts of Winter's school to learn more about the man her father intended for her. "Let's hear it," I snap.

"For starters, we have reason to believe Mr. Nyx escaped here from the Netherworld."

Gasps erupt through the suite as both Cedric and Abigail now stand at my sides. "Impossible!" Cedric exclaims, stepping in front of me.

"Oh it's very possible, I'm afraid." Dalcour's dark tone sends tremors through me, and fear grips me at what he'll say next. "Ever since their exile, the wicked Changeling witches have long sought more ways to open the gates of the Netherworld to the earthbound plane. And it seems they may have found their pawn in Nyx."

"I don't understand," Cedric begins, "While we supernaturals are still susceptible to a Changeling's advances, I thought their reach to mortals was limited?"

"Apparently, not as much as we've been led to believe. According to Nara, this may have all started with Melchior, Lord Elysian's son."

"How, my lord? Winter told me Melchior was lost at sea," I reply.

## Chapter Sixteen

"Perhaps." Dalcour's tone is more questioning than it is resolute. "When we were last here, Melchior mentioned he was on the cusp of a great find. If memory serves me, I believe he was looking for a golden obol. It was his hope the treasure could be used in the next antiquity auction during the cotillion. Even though I warned him that the search for such a treasure could prove disastrous, he insisted finding it would help ease some of the financial strain on his father and the estate. Knowing supernaturals would pay handsomely for it, Melchior made it his goal to find it. Unfortunately for him, I think he did."

"You think finding the obol somehow brought about the young Elysian's end?" Cedric asks.

"Even more, I think discovering the obol somehow brought Kharon Nyx into this world. What's worse, I am certain the witchery of the Changelings is behind it all!"

"Oh no!" Abigail shrieks, cupping her mouth with her hands. "So Nyx's intent is indeed nefarious?"

"I don't care what he or the Changelings want! If it brings even an ounce of harm to Winter and her family, I'll make them regret the day they crawled from their dark hole in the Netherworld!" I growl.

"That may be, young one," Dalcour cautions, with his hand now resting on my shoulder, "but I need to know something."

"What?" I snarl, my chest heaving in deep breaths as I work hard to keep my wolf at bay.

"Do you really love this woman as you say? I mean really love her—"

"With my whole heart," I declare, shaking his hand off me.

"I am glad to hear you say that. Because it's going to take every drop of love you have for her to do what is necessary to not only protect her from Kharon Nyx but also the sinister plans of the Changelings. So brace yourself, Lux. What you and Winter share is about to be put to the test."

"Then tell the Changelings to bring it on! Winter and I will pass with flying colors!"

# Chapter Seventeen

## *Winter*

For the second time today, my cousin Ross is eerily quiet. But this time, so is Rae. It doesn't take a genius to see I'm in a mood and they know all too well to just let me be.

While it's not a normal occurrence, the three of us have been privy to each other's diffidence over the years. Rae is usually the most subdued of us three. Her bouts of anger generally relate to the ill treatment of animals, global warming, and her abhorrence to the leisure use of plastic. Ross, on the other hand, usually suffers from some matter of the heart. Being one who is no stranger to both passion and heartbreak, while wearing his heart on his sleeve, any irritation to Ross can be laid back to the feet of some lackey or lumberman nearby.

Then there's me.

Not much gets me wound up, save my constant friction with my mother. Usually, however, it is my father to whom I look to for comfort. Not today. Even though he has always raised me with a stern hand, his open arms have always been there when I've needed him most. Although I had planned on sparing him the intimate details, I hoped to share my affection for Lux with my father. Of anyone on this island, it is my father's approval that matters most. And Lux will receive anything but approval from him.

As much as everything in me tells me I can yet trust Lux's sentiment and care toward me, I've also never known my father to lead me astray. While I have no desire to see Kharon Nyx as anything more than just another man on this island, what I learned about my family's history with wolves nullifies any possible future with Luxor Decanter.

Now, for the first time since Melchior's passing, my heart is broken.

Still, my heart cries desperately for Lux. Well beyond reason, I'm finding it hard to get him out of my mind—or off my hand! I scrubbed my palm

*Chapter Seventeen*

for thirty minutes trying to get his number off my skin to no avail. Neither alcohol nor lye soap are of any use.

"Win, I'm sorry, it's just not coming off," Rae softly says as she scrubs my palm for the fifth time.

"Argh!" I shriek, rubbing my hands feverishly into the hand towel in my bathroom.

"I'm sure it will fade away eventually," she offers, gently patting my back. A part of me is thankful for the gesture, but I also want to shake her hand off me. I'm not in the mood to be coddled.

Thankfully, my phone rings, interrupting the awkwardness building between us. "It's Clayton," Ross announces, handing me the phone. "He's probably returning your call about the last-minute seating changes."

"Good," I reply, quickly taking the phone from Ross. "Clayton, thanks for returning my call. Were you able to accommodate for the changes I sent you? My family will not have anyone else at our table. Keep the seating at five."

"Five?" Ross whispers back. "Remember, I'm bringing Stephen," he mumbles under a cupped hand as if he didn't want Rae to hear.

Rae chuckles and shakes her head. "As if I didn't see what time you snuck back into the house last night."

*One Winters Kiss*

"Yes, five," I repeat. "Stephen can have my seat," I add, tilting my chin away from the phone.

"What?" Both Ross and Rae protest in unison.

"Thank you, Clayton. Oh yes and tell Pam I'll be down shortly to check on the gift baskets for our guests. Thanks again, goodbye."

"Okay, hold the phone! What in tarnation do you mean, 'Stephen can have my seat?'" Ross blurts his words, leaning back into Rae's shoulder.

"You heard what I said. It's my job to see tonight's cotillion goes off without a hitch and I'll do so—behind the scenes." Pushing my way through the twins, I make my way back into my bedroom and quickly pull a sweater vest over my blouse.

"Hold on, Win," Rae starts, stepping in front of my view of myself in the mirror as I begin pulling my hair up into a bun. "Look, I still don't really understand what happened with you and this Lux guy, but don't let him cause you to miss something I know you've waited for since we were kids."

Rae may be right about one thing, this cotillion is something I've longed to see and experience. But I'll not put myself in any room with Luxor Decanter, any wolf, or supernatural being for that matter.

"You're right, Rae," I add, looking over her shoulder at a portion of my reflection in the mirror. Looking at myself, I see more of my

*Chapter Seventeen*

mother in me than usual. Turning quickly on my heel, I take Rae by the arm, smiling at the kind, small, caramel complexioned face with bright hazel eyes staring back at me through long sandy-brown bangs. Her sweet smile yanks my heart strings, but I muster strength to hold my ground. "But we were kids then, we're not now," I say, watching her hopeful eyes fall.

Before I have a chance to leave, Ross squares his place in front of me. Shaking his fore finger and head, with one hand on his hip, he stops in front of my doorway. "That may be, honey," Ross begins, his tone full of his typical sass. "But Rae didn't get the privilege of seeing you all wide-eyed and bushy tailed today. I, however, did see you. You were not simply smitten—no, honey—you were bitten by the love bug. A love bug of kinds of tall, dark and handsome! And those feelings, that I might add, I've never seen buzzing about you before, don't just go away."

Staring at Ross, tearful droplets threaten their release, but I force them aside. I don't have the luxury of crying right now.

"No, Ross those feelings don't just go away, but you know what else doesn't just go away? A father who insists on trying to force me with someone I don't love. I admit, I made a fool of myself with Lux but that doesn't mean I need to make a fool of myself with Kharon Nyx. I've had enough of playing the fool for one day. So what I will do is show my father that I can take care of not only this cotillion, but Elysian Manor without the help of a man at my side! I've never been a damsel in distress before and I don't intend on being one now. That's why I have no plan of playing dress up for some fairytale prince who doesn't exist."

Ross's mouth hangs open as he leans against the doorframe. This is third time I've rendered the almighty Ross Vereen speechless. *Who knew I had this power?* I inwardly pat my back.

"Now please, you and Rae, get dressed and prepare for the festivities. Tell that dashing Stephen of yours to treat you with the upmost respect," I say as my eyes well with more tears. "And Rae, I don't want you wasting another thought about a fool like Nyx that can't see you for the remarkable, kind-hearted soul you are. I am sure there will be plenty of desirable men of worth lining up to fill your dance card, you just make them work for it." With a wink to Rae and kiss to Ross's cheek, I slide past him and leave the room.

Before I cross the threshold, one lone tear falls to my cheek, and I am thankful I was able to make it out before the real waterworks began.

Walking down the stairs, finding my parents still at the base of the landing plummets my heart straight to the base of my stomach. It's been well over an hour since our last conversation and by

## Chapter Seventeen

the looks on their faces, it appears not much has changed.

"Winter, darling, where are you going?" Mother allows her sweet smile to spread over her face and I know she's working hard to soften the mood.

Father, on the other hand, is still wearing his stubbornness in full stride. "Yes, where are you going, young lady? You hardly look dressed for the festivities tonight."

"That's because I'm not going." The coolness of my tone meets my father just as I intended. He's not the only one with a little doggedness in this family. I can certainly dig my heel into the ground and plant it there if need be.

Looking down at my parents from the steps, I can sense the frustration brewing between them. I hate to be the cause for their apparent dissent, but soon they'll both have to learn I'm a grown woman who will not be controlled by them or anyone.

"Winter Elysian! Do you not understand your responsibilities? The Regency expects to see the Lady of Elysian Manor—and that is you!"

"Yes, father and they will see mother right at your side. I have duties to ensure the business of the evening are without incident and I will do just that. Not only do I need to ensure all of the art—"

"Oh rubbish!" My father exclaims. "I don't doubt you've managed every facet of tonight—but you have a staff of many to see to the minutia. You, young lady, have a place at my side."

"Well actually, sir, I was hoping your daughter would take her place beside me."

My heart rises back up to my chest but falls just as fast as its rising when I watch Kharon round the corner. Although he looks up at me with the warmest smile I've ever seen of him, nothing but disappointment fills the depths of me.

As much as I know I shouldn't give one thought about him, the only one I want to see right now is Lux. He's the only one I want. Period.

# Chapter Eighteen

## *Lux*

"Lord Marchand, are you going to tell us where we're going?"

All I want to do is find Winter. Instead, Dalcour is leading us to a wooded area near the shipyard. It's not quite where we departed the ferry when we first arrived, but it's not far from where all the sea vessels are docked.

Dalcour remains strangely quiet as we make our way through a thick brush of trees. Why he opts to keep us at a mundane mortal pace is beyond me. I could just as easily shift into my wolf and keep up with both he and Cedric as they take flight, but for some odd reason he keeps us on our feet.

What's worse, I notice Winter's scent is faint on this side of the island. I don't mind since it can only mean she doesn't frequent this area. With as eerie as this place feels, I'm glad she stays far from here.

But someone from her immediate has been here. I can smell it.

I've spent the day committing to memory not only Winter's scent, but both her father and cousin's pH levels are also locked in my senses. Despite how things have gone so far between Lord Elysian and me, I know once I make Winter my wife, she's not the only one I'll vow to protect. Her family will become my family. Having their scent etched in my memory, I know wherever they are, I'll keep them safe.

That is why I find the faint, yet distinct aroma of her family's essence prickling my pores in this grungy part of the woods disturbing. While I've never met her mom or her cousin Rae, from what Winter has shared about them, I highly doubt either woman would be caught out here.

"Stay quiet, Lux," Dalcour whispers over his shoulder, bringing one finger to his mouth. "We're almost there."

Despite having to discharge our weapons before coming onto the island, I'm not surprised to find my brother gripping our father's pocket blade close to his hip. A family heirloom, my brother never parts with it. Over the years he's managed

*Chapter Eighteen*

to evade airport security and even secret service agents, finding a way to keep our father's knife with him at all times. I'm not sure how he does it, nor have I ever bothered to ask, but I am thankful to see him with it as always.

Cedric casts wary glances to me as we make our way in front of a dark cave near a small stream of water. A rickety wooden boat with a long, wooden oar embroidered in silver subscript rests beside the stream leading to the cave.

"By the Order of Altrinion, what is this place!" Cedric mutters with a tight hold on his blade. Both his lips and mine curl with disgust as a poignant, musty odor muddles the crisp air. "What is that smell?"

"It smells like—"

"Death." Dalcour finishes my sentiment before I can utter the words.

"What is this place, my lord?" I question, looking around, wary of what or who may be lurking in the woods.

"This is Kharon's cave," Dalcour says darkly. "It is where you must go, young one. Alone."

Jumping in front of me, Cedric throws his arm across my chest, preventing a move I have yet to take. "I'm sorry, my lord, I'll not allow it. Send me instead!"

"Brother, please." Tugging at his arm, he keeps his frame pushed against me. "I've got to do this!"

"Do what? Lord Marchand has yet to tell us! I'll not send my brother into that hellhole with nothing save the first fluttering of his heart. No! Not on my watch!"

Placing his hand on my brother's shoulder, Dalcour offers a consoling smile. "Cedric, I'm afraid, there's nothing you can do about it. This task is for Lux and Lux alone."

"And what, my lord, is this task? Please, don't send him in there blindly!"

Looking over my brother's arm, Dalcour locks eyes with me and points toward the cave. "Lux, what is in that cave is what you'll need to conquer to ensure Kharon never marries Winter."

"Fine! Whatever it is, I'll go and get it."

"We'll get it together!" Cedric adds, pounding his fist to my chest.

"No!" Dalcour lashes back, pulling Cedric away from me. "He may be your younger brother, Cedric, but Lux must do this on his own. It is his love alone for Winter that will forge through whatever darkness lies within the walls of that cave. Just as you risked your very life and stood in the bloody pools of the taming wells until the monstrous thirst of your beloved Abigail was lifted, so must Lux withstand whatever lot befalls him. He must do this alone."

Circling Dalcour, I make my way back to Cedric's side and take a firm hold of his back. "It's

## Chapter Eighteen

all right brother, I'll be fine. I love Winter more than my own life. Whatever I must contend, I will defeat. Whatever I must obtain, I will. I'll do what I have to, brother. Even if I have to fight you—I'll go to whatever end to ensure she is mine."

At my admission, I watch as pride swells my brother's chest and a small, yet appreciative grin hovers over the tightened lines of his bronzed jaw. "Ah! So you do love her. I never thought I'd see the day when your heart would be carted by love's carriage. But it is certainly a sight to behold! I am happy for you, brother. Now, go do what you must to make Winter your bride."

"Yes, brother, I'll do just that!"

"Please, make it fast, will you, brother! I'd much rather meet my sister-in-law than to stand in the stench of this bog another minute."

Laughing, I shake my head, knowing my brother's jokes do little to hide the concern I spy lingering behind his eyes. Still, I don't have long to admire his care for me when Lord Marchand quickly turns me back to him.

"Before you enter, I'll tell you this, the obol of Kharon is held by Changeling magic. You know well the deceit, trickery, and witchery of their kind. Believe nothing their lies reveal. Trust your heart. Trust the love you have for Winter and she for you. Trust nothing else. Once you're in there, only you, and you alone, can bring resolution to the warring of both your heart and mind. It is then you will obtain the one thing to seal you and Winter's fate. Do you understand?"

"Yes, my lord." My words are quick as I turn on my heel and make my way to the entrance of the cave.

"You can do this, brother," I hear Cedric call to me from behind. I don't take time to turn to see his face, but the care in his tone gives me all the confidence I need to go forward.

*"Yes, I can,"* I whisper to myself as the rank odor thickens as I walk deeper into Kharon's lair.

Small cackling sounds surround me as my eyes adjust to the murky darkness inside. Menacing, hyena-like growls cause the hairs on my forearm to stand and my muscles to tense, wary of whatever lurks in burrow of this deathly hole.

Dark gray smoke fills the space around me, making the air almost suffocating. Still, I work hard to keep my senses about me with my fists locked at my sides, ready for whatever comes next.

*"Weary soul, lost and alone, searching for one to make his home. Love he seeks now with haste; his own heart break will seal his fate."* The slithering yet sultry musings of two voices harmoniously speaking as one ring aloud throughout the cave. While I can't see any faces looming through their smoky veil, the ominous

## Chapter Eighteen

tingle now prickling my pores tells me all I need to know about who and what is talking to me.

The Changelings.

Long have wolves like me been warned of the dark duplicity of the Changelings witches. Ever since Orion, of the Dunes Paw pack was deceived by their kind, bringing the curse of the moon upon his kin—I've been careful to avoid the snares these dark ones set.

"Trust nothing else," I repeat Dalcour's final words under my breath, closing my eyes as I see the smoke shift before me. "Trust your heart, Lux, your heart," I mumble, stretching my hands out in front of me.

As I do, the texture of a wet, cold stone freezes the tips of my fingers. Opening my eyes, the thick gray smoke hovers over the space in front of me and a shadowy dark haze covers the tall stone, blocking my view. Looking at the mysterious fume, shapes form and I now see Winter standing with Kharon in front of the manor.

A loud roar bellows through me as I watch Kharon take Winter's wrist, kissing her hand. Bashfully covering her smile like she did with me earlier today, she laughs as he loops his arm through hers, leading her away from the mansion.

Screaming her name, I work hard to resist the urge to shift and make my way back to the manor. Once more, the Changelings shrilling, cackling shriek echoes through the cave and I reach my hand through the mist, but the images change just as I do.

This time what I see, puppeteers the marionette strings I now know only Winter holds. Kharon's bulking arms are now wrapped around her waist as the two dance merrily with Lord Elysian's affirming smile hovering in the distance. But it's the endearing look of her eyes as the two embrace stirring a frenzy in my heart.

"No! No!" I shout, hitting my fists against the tall freezing stone. A cold wind whips through the cave, but it's not until I feel an icy diamond stinging my cheekbone that I know the pain of heartbreak. Another lone tear cradles itself in the corner of my eye and for the first time I wonder if what Winter and I shared was ever real.

*"Now he sees, now he knows. Broken hearts seal his soul. Darkness, sorrow, no love bloom. Never to mate, snared by doom."* Once more the wicked liturgy of the Changelings resounds through the dark cave, and I bang my hands against the cold stone again.

*Trust nothing else. Trust your heart.* Thoughts of Dalcour's words ring aloud in my forlorn mind, reviving the broken pieces of my heart.

A low, thumping beat reverberates through my chest as even my wolf rages within me, beckoning me to recall the sweetness of Winter's kiss, the

## Chapter Eighteen

way she felt in my arms, and the moment I told her I wanted her to be my wife.

I know what we shared was no fleeting encounter. What we shared was real.

It is real.

Growling, a loud roar bellows through me as I shout Winter's name and the foggy gray haze before me slowly fades.

*"The heart, deceitful above all. Stray to love, will surely fall. Lest you—"*

"No! I'll not hear another word of your dark witchery! I'll hear no more lies!" I shout, turning about the cave. Again, their shrieking laughter resonates throughout the cave, but I've grown tired of their trickery. "Winter loves me, that much is true! Do what you will to me, but you'll never take away the one thing your hollow souls can never understand. True love."

Just then, a loud whistling wind whips through the cave, sending a glacial gale force around the entirety of the dark burrow. A small light from beyond the cave pierces through the darkness and the icy stone before me begins to melt.

Looking over my shoulder, I see my brother and Lord Marchand standing at the clearing of the cave. Dutifully as ever, I am thankful to see both men still waiting for me on the other side of the darkness I just endured.

Small, appreciative smiles glaze over their faces as they regard me. But it's their now widened eyes and parted lips that give me pause as they peer over my shoulder.

A tinge of fear stings my heart as thoughts of the wretched return of the Changelings freezes me still.

"No, it can't be!" Dalcour gasps as he steps just over the threshold of the cave. "My word, it is," he adds, looking past me with disbelief.

My brother remains frozen with his mouth gaped open. With his hands down at his sides and not at the holster of his blade, a modicum of comfort quiets the gnawing fear of the Changeling's return.

Heaving a heap of air, I slowly turn back around, following Dalcour's eyes as he looks behind me.

But I am not prepared for what I see.

Now I understand what Dalcour meant. Because what my eyes now behold, changes everything.

## Chapter Nineteen

*Winter*

"Your timing is as impeccable as always, Kharon! Now, would you please talk some sense into Winter," Father sighs, exhausted. Leaning heavy on his cane, he shifts his weight from his bad knee, grimacing. Mother glances at him, worry filling her face, but he looks away from her, keeping his attention on me and Kharon. I love my father, but he's too stubborn to even give himself the relief he needs.

"Ah, well, I'm sure Winter has enough sense all her own," Kharon adds with a wink and smile toward me. "But I wouldn't mind resuming our conversation from earlier if she doesn't mind."

*One Winters Kiss*

Shocked to hear Kharon call me by my name, my mouth hangs open slightly surprised.

"She doesn't mind at all!" Mother exclaims, not giving me a chance to reply.

"Yes, please, Kharon, I'm sure talking with you will do her some good," Father grumbles, limping toward his study, shaking his head and mumbling along the way. Mother keeps at his heel as he exits, smiling at Kharon and issuing me a daring glare as she makes her way out of the foyer.

"I'm sorry, Kharon, but I really need to get to the ballroom. There are quite a few things I need to tend to in preparation for tonight," I say, trotting down the steps.

"Of course, I understand. I'll just walk you outside then," Kharon adds, making his way to open the door for me.

Holding the door wide, a nervous smile crosses his face as I pass him, and I realize it's the same nervousness I saw in him earlier. Kharon is always so sure and steady, it's actually quite odd seeing him the least bit rattled.

"Look, Kharon," I start, ready to simply get the elephant out of the room. Turning quickly, I'm not prepared to find Kharon so close to me as we stand on the large cobble stone landing of the manor.

"Yes, Winter," he answers softly. His steely stare locks with mine and the desperation I see

## Chapter Nineteen

dancing behind his eyes as he looks back at me takes me by surprise.

Stepping back, I laugh, holding my hand over my face wondering what strange celestial event is in the works causing the men around me to act this way. I suppose I've grown so accustomed to all the burly lumberjacks, foul mouthed fishermen, and grumpy old men on the island, I'm not usually the recipient of swooning suitors.

*Must be a full moon.*

And just that fast, my thoughts drift back to Lux. Fond memories of being in his arms, seeing him naked, and our first kiss stir longings within me I thought for sure I scrubbed away as I tried to remove his number from my palm. Looking at my hand, I see faint markings of his writing between the lines of my palm, and I can't help smiling at the thought of Luxor Decanter.

"Win?" Kharon says my name once more, taking me by the wrist and kissing my opposite hand.

Both his unwanted kiss and the immediate shortening of my name bring me back to the moment. Pulling my hand from his grasp, I remind myself neither Kharon nor Lux are a part of my plan. My only goals are to show my parents I can handle the business of the manor without any man. I don't have time to indulge fantasies of men who only want me to escape supernatural curses or who only want to start a family with me because it checks off some old-fashioned to-do list.

"Look, Kharon, what I was going to say was that I'm sorry I ran off on you this morning."

"Well, I'm glad to hear you say that because I thought we could pick up where we left off," Kharon says with a broad smile that stretches from ear to ear.

"I don't think so, Kharon," I begin, taking the iron railing in my hand as I make my way down the steps.

"Win?" Taking my wrist, Kharon stops me from continuing down the steps. Leaning toward me, Kharon takes my chin gently in his hand. "What's wrong? Did I do something to upset you?"

Slowly pulling myself from his palm, I shake my head and take one step down to make a bit more separation between us. "It's not you, Kharon, it's me. I'm only apologizing because I didn't mean to be rude, but not because I wanted to see what was in that little velvet box of yours."

There, I said it. *Elephant released.*

"Ah, that," Kharon chuckles, throwing his head back with a sly smile. "Well, Win, what did you think was in that box?" Confused, I take a few more steps down the stairs until I reach the bottom. Kharon keeps up with me, tugging my arm gently to keep my attention. "Perhaps I should show you."

*Chapter Nineteen*

"No, Kharon, I don't think that's necessary," I begin as I watch him fumble through his pockets. Pulling out the small velvet box, the corners of Kharon's mouth curve upward, moving slowly with his eyes.

"See, take a look," he says, opening the box.

"It's empty," I reply stunned. I notice something like black sand inside, but I'm happy it's not a ring.

"Well, yes, at least for now, Win," he answers darkly, returning to his normal deep gaze.

"I—I—um—I don't know what to—"

"It's okay, Win. So that we are clear, yes, I did speak to your father of marriage. But I only did so out of a means of respect. I didn't want your father to think I had any wayward thoughts about you. Please know, Win, I understand that we don't really know one another, but today I wanted to talk to you about the two of us officially taking the time to at least get to know one another. And then, maybe, one day, after some time, you'll be okay with the idea of something going in this box. Today, however, I only wanted to start at the beginning."

Surprise swells the walls of my chest as my eyes dart between Kharon and the small box in his large palm. This is not what I expected.

And it still isn't what I wanted---at least not with Kharon.

"Kharon, I don't know what to say."

"It's okay, Win, you don't have to say anything right now, but I didn't want to let this day go without telling you how I feel."

My mouth parts once more, but this time a strong wind blows through the courtyard, I faintly hear what sounds like a snarling howl from the distance. A shivering tingle ripples through me and memories of Lux's growl stir through the depths of me.

Kharon shifts himself so that he is in front of me as I begin looking around the courtyard, curious if Lux is nearby. Gazing quickly over Kharon's shoulder, I look around but only notice some of the grounds people and staff, mulling about.

"Are you okay, Winter?" Kharon says, regaining my attention.

"When did you start calling me Winter?" Kharon seems a bit off kilter. He's all over the place.

"Oh, do you not prefer it? So now you see why I said I wanted us to take some time to get to know one another. I certainly don't want to misstep; least of all with your name." He smiles back at me, widening his arm to loop with mine.

"Well, to be honest I prefer Winter."

"Perfect! Now we're off to a good start!" He laughs, leading us toward the ballroom entrance.

*Chapter Nineteen*

"Kharon, look I can appreciate you wanting to get to know me, but what if that's not what I want. I mean I think you are a very nice man but I'm really not interested in exploring more than friendship with you."

He looks stunned. Like a deer in headlights. A man like Kharon is certainly not accustomed to being denied.

"Well tell me, Winter who is it that you'd like to explore something beyond friendship with?"

*"Who?"* I repeat back, watching his posture stiffen.

"Please don't tell me it's that wretched mongrel seeking to usurp your affluence for his own. I'd hate to see you taken advantage of." The tenor of Kharon's tone is now darker, not as light as earlier.

"What do you know about Lux?" I ask, surprised. When did my father have a chance to tell Kharon?

"I was there when that mangy beast berated your father, demanding he give you to him and his pack. He made quite a spectacle of himself before your father had him removed from the island."

"Removed? What! When?"

"I'll just say it's all for your best, Winter. Nothing good would come of such a cursed soul. But he is long gone from here now. He was last seen heading toward the final ferry for the mainland some time ago."

"*He's gone?*" A sickening sadness sweeps through my soul. Despite knowing my father and Kharon are probably right about Lux, the thought of him being gone grieves parts of me only awakened by the first kiss we shared. Whether my affection for him be folly, I don't know. What I do know is, in the short time we spent together, I never loved anyone like Lux Decanter.

And in this moment, I know, I never will again.

# Chapter Twenty

*Lux*

"What are we waiting for? We need to get to Lord Elysian and Winter!" I shout to my brother and Lord Marchand as they discuss options of bringing our recent reveal to light.

"Steady yourself, young one," Dalcour warns as I near the entrance of the cave. Making his way in front of me before I can exit, he holds me firm at the shoulders, shaking his head. "You can't just go marching into the ballroom like this Lux. Your brash behavior earlier nearly got you thrown off the island. If Lord Elysian even sees you like this, how will you plead your case?"

"Plead my case? Why, my lord all the evidence to my case is right here, melting in our very presence!" I snap back, pointing over my shoulder.

"Yes, brother, but Lord Marchand is right, a cooler head is best in this situation."

"Fine, Cedric! But if you two think I'm going to stand by idly while Winter's father marries her off to that ferryman—"

"It won't come to that! I promise you," Dalcour gently replies. "Just please follow my lead."

"We will," Cedric answers for me, wrapping his arm around my neck. "What do you need us to do?"

"Get off me, Cedric," I say, pushing myself out from under my brother's tight hold. "And yes, my lord, I trust your leading."

Dalcour smiles back at me while he paces the floor, holding his hand to his chin. "Well, Cedric if you don't mind, I'll head over to the ballroom and take Abigail with me. I'll look less conspicuous. That way, she can keep a close eye on Winter while I keep Lord Elysian occupied. You two go back to your suite and get yourselves together. Yes, Lux, you'll need to change your attire. When you stand before Lord Elysian again, he needs to see you at your best."

"Oh, because what I'm wearing now doesn't quite hit the mark?" I laugh, pointing to my borrowed lumberman attire.

## Chapter Twenty

"Not even close, brother," Cedric sighs, with his hand covering his face, chuckling as he turns away from me.

Pointing behind Dalcour, I need to understand what Dalcour plans to do with our recent discovery. "And what about—"

"Well, young one, the only way to prove your intent is by revealing everything to Winter and her family. You'll have both my word and your brother backing you up every step of the way."

"Lord Marchand is right, Lux. Besides, what you've discovered in Kharon's cave is enough for any father to relent of any plan to pair his daughter with such a duplicitous soul."

"That brings up another point. What will become of Kharon when the Elysian's learn the truth?" I ask.

"According to legend, the ferryman must keep his obol with him at all times. Now that we have what he's bound the obol to and the source of his magic, you'll need only one thing to finally rid Winter and her family of his treachery once and for all."

"What more does he need, my lord?" Cedric questions, casting a worried glance over his shoulder to me.

"It doesn't matter, Cedric. Whatever it is, I'll do it." Although I'm surprised there's more I need to do, I didn't come this far to give up on my future with Winter.

"I'm glad to hear you say that, but I think this task will be a bit more enjoyable. All you need is to kiss the woman you love."

"My lord? I don't understand."

"Legends of old state the ferryman was cursed by a coin and deprived of love. However, if he should ever gain wealth and a love to call his own, he would be free of his curse. If I had to guess, his obol carries the magic of the Changelings and as such they would've bound the obol to something of this world in order to maintain his appearances. Now that you've found what he's using to bind himself to an earthbound existence, only your kiss—a true love's kiss between you and Winter can bring a finality to his schemes, effectively freeing the Elysian's from his hold."

"Well, brother, I do hope what you and Winter share is true."

Thinking of the first time I saw Winter, I knew then she was the woman for me. I knew in that moment she and I were destined to be together. She's not only my mate. She's my everything.

"In almost three hundred years I can say I've never known a love as true."

Both Cedric and Dalcour lock their eyes with mine, smiling, yet still slightly surprised by my admission. Over the years, I've scoffed at the mere thought of love, now here I am risking all that I am for the woman I love.

# Chapter Twenty-One

*Winter*

Even though Kharon made me promise to save him a dance before he left me earlier, I have no intent on obliging his request. I have neither interest in him or in this ball knowing Lux is not here.

I know I shouldn't sulk over a man who was only trying to trick me, but my heart remains firm that what we shared was real. As much as I try to push thoughts of Lux aside, memories of the short time we spent together are on constant replay in my mind.

His touch. His eyes. His smile. His kiss.

Everything about Luxor Decanter has me so out of sorts I can barely think. I guess that's why I'm forcing myself to work alongside my staff tonight instead of enjoying the festivities. I can only hope keeping busy will prove useful in keeping Lux off my mind and out of my heart.

Although I've spent years daydreaming what it would feel like to dance among the supernaturals during our cotillion, the thought of doing so without Lux here is too painful to ponder. Even more, I'll be just as happy when this whole thing is over, and they are off the island.

"Cassidy, can you open up the second room for coat checks? The first room is getting full," I say as I hand two minks to one of the student attendants.

"Yes, ma'am," Cassidy chuckles nervously, grabbing the keys from the drawer.

She looks up at me, bashful, before glancing over her shoulder at the handsome young man she's been making googly eyes with for the last fifteen minutes. While it doesn't hurt to be sure the second coat closet is open, I'm more interested in breaking up whatever is happening between her and the striking brunette she can't keep her eyes off of.

Looking at him and the flash of his golden eyes, reminiscent of Lux, I am sure he is also a wolf. The last thing we need is another mortal being caught up by the wiles of wolves who want us for

## Chapter Twenty-One

nothing more than saving themselves from their wretched curse.

"Oh, well, I guess since Cinderella isn't going to the ball, she doesn't want anyone to have fun," I hear Ross chides me as he walks down the long corridor.

Although I want to jab him back for his snide remark, I cannot. I'm too awestruck at how amazing he looks. Not that I'm surprised, but my cousin really cleans up well. Wearing a fitted winter white tux with a poofy peppermint stripped tie, he is the epitome of all things Christmas.

"Oh my! What happened to the dude in ripped jeans and the Tupac tee from this morning?" I laugh, watching Ross spin in front of me, showing off his tailored look.

"What's the saying, the suit making the man? I think in this case it's the man making the suit," Ross adds, pulling at his collar, posing.

"Well, I'm afraid you'll have to head to the foyer outside of the ballroom to get your close-up Mr. Demille!" I tease, shaking my head.

"Ah yes, a close up because I am certainly the photogenic one in the family, that's for sure!" Looking at himself in the floor length mirror along the wall, Ross vogues, alternating poses. He's such a ham.

"More like the vain one," I counter, shaking my head. "Where is your date?" I ask, attempting to divert his attention from himself.

"Oh Stephen is in the little boy's room primping. He said something about his gel to mousse ratio being a bit off. I told him he looked darling, but I suppose he wanted to match my swagger," Ross adds, twirling his fingers through his curly mane hanging at his forehead.

"Of course," I wink back. "But where is your better half? Where is Rae?" I say, peering down the corridor for any sign of his twin.

"Yeah, about that, I don't think she'll make it," Ross replies, with his head low.

"What? Why not? We spent weeks picking out the perfect gown."

"I'm afraid she saw you and Kharon arm and arm in front of the manor earlier. She's just not feeling it."

"Oh no! Look, she needs to know nothing happened between me and Kharon. He only walked me over here. Besides, I told him I'm not interested in him."

"You did? But what about his proposal?"

"Apparently, he wasn't planning to propose to me earlier. He said he wanted to see if I was interested in starting a relationship with him. I told him that wasn't what I wanted. So look, if Rae wants him, she needs to go after it. She'll get no interference from me. I even told my parents the same."

## Chapter Twenty-One

"Wow! Look at you owning your heart!" Ross dashes an admiring smile as he bumps his shoulder into mine. "Yeah, but you know Rae, she'll probably lay low for the evening. She doesn't want to get caught in the middle—especially with Uncle El. You know once he digs his heels in, he's pretty much cemented in the ground. So while I know you think the door on Kharon is shut, I doubt your parents feel the same; least of all Uncle Elysian."

"Did someone mention me?" I hear my father's hearty chuckle round the corner of the coat check booth. He and my mom are a handsome pair. My father's tux is impeccably tailored, making even his rotund frame a bit more taut. Mother, on the other hand, is jaw-droppingly stunning! Her flowy red gown with a slit at the top of her knee shows off her ridiculously girlish figure to a tee. With her long brown hair draped to one side of her shoulder, she could easily pass more as my sister than my mother.

Although their romance may not have been the fairytale, romantic story I'd been led to believe, I have no doubt, my father indeed took one look at my mother and offered her the world. By the way the pride swells his chest as he walks at her side, it's apparent she still makes him weak in the knees.

That's what I want…one day. I thought I could have that with Lux, but I was wrong.

"Uncle and Auntie, you two look marvelous!" Ross exclaims, lifting his phone to take a few candid pictures.

"Oh Ross, please!" Mother waves her hand across her chest, blushing. It's good to see her relaxed.

"So am I to believe you'll remain out here all evening, young lady?" My father asks, leaning into me across the counter with one brow raised.

"Darling," Mother admonishes him, pulling her paper fan out from her clutch. "Winter has made her choice. If she wants to come to the ball, she can. If not, that is her choice. We must respect it."

Surprised, I can hardly believe what I just heard. Either she's trying to be the broker of peace, or she truly understands how I feel. Whatever her reason, I am thankful.

"Thanks, mom," I whisper back. Nodding with her eyes only, she leans toward me and offers her cheek. Kissing her warm face, the sadness that once held my heart slowly fades. Even though my mother is often hard on me, I think she knows I can take care of myself.

"Fine, fine! I'll let it go." Father grumbles tossing his hands up in surrender. "As long as you know I'll only ever do what I believe is in your best interests, my sweet girl." Resting his hand on top

## Chapter Twenty-One

of mine, my father's eyes search my face and I offer a smile in return, hopeful he'll understand I'm okay.

"And here he is ladies and gentlemen, looking like a tall glass of Merlot!" Ross exclaims, clapping his hands as he sees Stephen walk down the hall. Stephen's face turns blushing red as he makes his way toward us. More burly than my lanky cousin, Stephen's bulking frame seems to take up the tight corridor.

Looking swelt in his dark maroon tux, I watch Ross's eyes beam as Stephen's curly hair cascades along his strong jawline. Ross quickly loops his arm through his date as if he feared someone might swoop him away. I can't say I blame him. He cleans up pretty good for a lumberjack.

"You both look nice!" Mother says, giving Stephen a light peck on the cheek.

"Thank you, Auntie Vivian! We aim to please," Ross follows with a bow at his waist.

"But where is Rae?" Mother asks.

"Um, she's back at the manor. Once I'm done seeing to the hostess gifts, she and I are going to hang out. You know a girl's night," I quickly state before Ross has a moment to share. It's not a total lie. I do have every intent on spending the evening with my cousin tonight. I need her to know there's nothing between me and Kharon and if nothing else we have each other.

"That's nice, Win," Mother interjects, beating my father to the punch. I'm sure not having his entire family at the cotillion tonight doesn't sit well with him. Still, I'm thankful for my mom reining in my father's rebuke.

"Well, we should make our way inside," Father mumbles, drawing his lips into a thin line. Ross blares his eyes at me, blowing out an air of relief as he and Stephen follow my parents down the corridor.

Just as they leave, my hostess team assembles themselves along the hall. Each person has a white gift box with a red bow in their hand, ready to present to the supernatural regency as they arrive. At every cotillion, the human nobles of the regency make it their tradition to present gifts to the supernaturals. Over the years gifts have been as simple as wine and cheese baskets or even blankets. This year, I decided on something different. Glass ornaments for the sixteen-foot pine adorning the center of the ballroom. I even designed a special silver snowflake at the lumbermill as a tree topper. One lucky guest will have the honor of topping this year's tree.

It was my idea to have the factions trim the tree together at the end of the evening. I thought the gesture would be a symbol of all of us, both mortal and supernatural, coming together as one. My father thought it was a great idea. Too bad I have no intention of seeing how it turns out.

# Chapter Twenty-Two

*Lux*

"How do I look, brother?"

"For the fifth time, you look good Lux," Cedric sighs, leaning back into the chair with his arms folded.

"Are you sure? You heard Lord Marchand; I need to present myself better than I did before with Lord Elysian." Jerking my bowtie to the side, I fuss with the thin collar of my shirt and keep working the tie.

"You look fine, brother," Cedric grumbles, getting up from his seat and walking toward me. "But if you take any longer the stone may fully melt. I'm pretty sure that'll put a damper in your reunion with Winter." Swatting my hands from the bowtie, Cedric adjusts the tie around my neck, tapering it neatly along my collar. "Now what about me?" He asks with his hands outstretched.

"Well, all I'll say is I'll make other sleeping arrangements tonight," I laugh, stepping back to admire my ever-stylish big brother. Donned in a classic black tux, the athletic cut shows off his brawn just as he intended.

"What do you mean?" Cedric asks, raising an eyebrow as he leans down to tighten the laces of his shoe.

"I'm sure after my sister-in-law takes one look at you in that ensemble, this suite will be off limits and I'll be persona non grata. It's bad enough when I have to endure your normal amount of swooning, but my poor sister-in-law will be beside herself when she sees you!"

"Ah! You're just saying that because I helped you carry that freezing stone out of Kharon's cave!"

"Perhaps," I laugh, playfully shoving my brother's back. "But you bring up a good point, I really don't want to lug that thing around in my suit. How should we handle that?"

"Already on it, brother." Nodding at me with his typical smirk he starts texting. "I've instructed Dranoel to assemble a few members of the Guard from patrol to take the task of holstering the stone."

*Chapter Twenty-Two*

"You see, that's why you're the big brother! You always have foresight. I really admire that about you."

"What did you say?" Cedric tilts his head, surprised. "Did you just pay me a compliment? Are you well, brother? First love now compliments. This woman is really whipping you into a tailspin!"

"I'm trying to be serious," I mumble back, rolling my eyes. Cedric, more than anyone, knows this isn't easy for me.

"I know, and I'm enjoying it. Continue," Cedric laughs, gesturing his hand toward me.

"Look, brother, this is new territory for me. This whole love thing. I feel crazy. Crazier than I've ever felt in my life. It's like when I shift how my emotions are amuck when I'm in between the wolf and this form—but a thousand times worse. I've never felt so out of sorts. Is this how you feel? Will it always be like this?"

Letting out a hearty chuckle, Cedric leans against the wall, with his arms folded. "Calm yourself, Lux." His amusement of my erratic emotions isn't lost on me. "Listen, what you feel for her is normal. But you're also a wolf so your need to protect and be with her is unlike any other."

"So this is normal?" Frustration brews within me like a steaming cup of espresso.

Pushing away from the wall, he rests his large palm on my shoulder. "No brother, this is love."

Cedric squeezes my shoulder, narrowing his eyes, ensuring I get the message.

I do.

The flustering feelings bubbling within me now feel like chaotic nervous energy. I want to scream, shift, run for miles, lift Winter in my arms, and claim her as my own in all one swift motion. But she deserves better. We deserve better. And I plan on giving her nothing but the best of me.

All of me.

Shaking his head as he smiles, Cedric pulls his tight grip from me and saunters to the kitchen. "I only hope my dear wife left something in here for me," he fusses, looking through the refrigerator.

"Feeding time, is it?" I almost forgot.

"We're way past the hour, I'm afraid," he answers, turning back toward me with two large bottles of blood. "I'm famished."

"Now see, if you'd chosen to embrace your wolf like me, you wouldn't be hostage to bloodlust."

Shrugging his shoulders, Cedric places both bottles in the microwave to warm the contents.

"Just a few steaks, burgers, and the occasional deer or other forest creature, from time to time is all a wolf needs for sustenance. Human food and little woodland delight do the trick for me," I mock, watching my brother guzzle down the first bottle.

"I suppose, but then again you're forgetting my true reason why I'm a vampire. It is for that reason

## Chapter Twenty-Two

I'll do whatever I have to for Abigail. Because that, my brother, is what love requires. True love requires you to sacrifice your own will for the woman you love. You see it was the love I had for Abigail that made me what I am. I purposely withstood the taming wells, holding her hand during hours of bloodletting for no other reason than I wanted her to know I'd be with her through it all. I did it all for her." Keeping his eyes locked on me as he lifts the second bottle to his mouth and the weight of his words sits like an elephant on my chest.

I love who and what I am. I love being a wolf. My brother gave all of that up for Abigail. As much as I know Winter is the one for me, can I honestly say I'd give up being a wolf for her? That's a question I hope I'll never have to answer.

"So do you now understand, Lux? When you say you love this woman, you have to truly mean it. You have to be willing to lay it all on the line for her. And she must be able to do the same for you. Being Altrinion, my bloodlust is not as insatiable as Abigail, a mortal-made vampire. Daily, she has to tame her tongue. Not just so she doesn't become some rogue Scourge vampire, but so she can walk at my side. We don't exist in the shadows. We live among mortals—share in this world of civility that Lord Marchand is working so hard to create. For that reason, every day she denies her thirsts and urges, bending her will to binge from a bottle rather than tear the throat of some unsuspecting mortal, for no other reason than her love for me. Do you understand, brother?"

Swallowing the thick knot in my throat, I force aside any measure of doubt. Although I can't describe it as surely as Cedric does of his love for Abigail, my heart knows the love me and Winter have is true.

# Chapter Twenty-Three

*Winter*

"Cassidy, are you sure you'll be fine?" This lovesick teen is in awe of every supernatural creature entering the hall. First, she had her eyes set on the brunette wolf, but when an entourage of other young adults made an appearance, she turned her focus elsewhere. Now Cassidy can't keep her sights off a thunderous stallion with bronzed skin and long sandy dreads. Looking at him, I have no doubt he's an Altrinion Vampire, but something tells me despite all his grandeur, he's not the one in charge.

I've been at the front concierge desk for almost an hour and I've yet to see Lord Dalcour Marchand. All the gossips say he's the most alluring of his kind, with a stately, enigmatic lure that makes knees buckle and mouths drool. While I suppose he may be all those things, I can't picture anyone parrying the pull of Lux Decanter.

At least not in my mind.

But I'll have to forgo seeing Lord Marchand and push past my pain of losing Lux just as quickly as I got him. Now is not the time. Now is the time to be with Rae. I'll not let her sulk alone. If Kharon can't see past my father's guises enough to see just how wonderful my beautiful cousin is, he doesn't deserve her. She deserves better.

And that starts with a cousin who cares for her and her feelings.

"Yes, I'll be okay," Cassidy answers with a laugh taking my hand in hers. "Besides, Russell and the rest will be here to keep me company once the rest of the guests have arrived. So go ahead and get your girl's night with Rae going." Lightly turning me around, Cassidy pushes my back, laughing as she forces me to exit from behind the desk.

"All right, well, please call me if you need anything. Promise!" I say, turning back around, looking to see if I missed anything.

"Scout's honor!" she says with two crossed fingers raised. "Now go!"

## Chapter Twenty-Three

"Okay, okay," I shake my head, turning quickly on my heel.

"Leaving so soon, Lady Elysian?" a dark, lush voice startles me, causing me to stumble off the step. "Whoa, I've got you."

Looking up, I finally see him. Lord Marchand. With his strong hands now on my arms, I am now face to face with the man I've only heard about in passing. From his dewy, pecan complexion to his almond-shaped eyes with a crimson hue, he is every bit as decadent as he's been described.

And yet, nothing.

He is not Lux.

"I'm sorry to frighten you, my lady." He offers a broad, handsome smile as he takes my hand, helping me settle myself.

"Oh, I—I, um—thank you for catching me, my lord." I sound like a rambling fool. *Pull yourself together, Winter.*

"You're quite all right, Lady Elysian. I think doing nothing would be rude and I would not want to be impolite to my hostess."

"Your hostess? Oh, I'm sorry, you must have me confused with my mother, Vivian. I'm her dau—"

"Yes, you are the Lady Winter Elysian. Am I correct?" he finishes my words, still smiling wide.

"Um yes." My nerves are on edge. But when I find the smile of a beautiful woman at his side, my anxiousness settles.

"And she is every bit as lovely as Lux described. Isn't she, Lord Marchand?" the beautiful woman says with a bright smile that reaches her eyes.

"Lux?" I whisper, stepping back.

"Yes, she is. It is no wonder he is quite taken with her," he nods to his companion.

"I'm sorry, Lord Marchand, what do you know about Lux?" I thought Lux was gone. When did he have time to talk to anyone about me and of all people why would he tell Lord Marchand?

Looking at me as though I said I joke, both he and the woman chuckle, sharing glances with each other.

"Well, Lady Elysian as the leader of the supernatural regency, it does me good to know everyone within my purview, don't you think? But that's not what you want to know, is it? You want to know if Lux is still on the island."

"What? Um—" Either I'm that obvious or he can read my mind.

"Well, my lady, when you start your school, you'll want to ensure your students learn quickly that Altrinions can read minds," he adds, tapping his temple. "But that is a topic for another time. Perhaps then I can talk at length with you about your ambitions."

As he speaks, I vaguely recall father mentioning how some supernaturals can read minds, but I can't remember if he specifically referred to Altrinions. Lux was right, having supernaturals as

## Chapter Twenty-Three

a part of the school would mean a world of difference.

Still, I don't give myself time to ponder goals for the school, when there are more pressing matters to discuss.

"Is he gone?" I softly ask, fearful of his response.

"No, Winter. He's still here and he's on his way to see you."

Butterflies swarm my insides, and the pacing of my heart quickens. Just hearing Lux is still on the island sends my emotions into overdrive. I need to work hard to keep my composure. Although, from the look on Lord Marchand's face I know he sees the cartwheels I'm doing in my mind.

"He is?" I choke out the two words as if my mouth was full of peanut butter.

"Yes, Winter, and he can't wait to see you," the woman says, taking my hand in hers. Despite her long black satin gloves, the icy touch of her fingers lets me know she is a vampire. While I've been taught to be careful around the mortal made Scourge vampires like this woman, the caring regard in her sea blue eyes tells me I have nothing to fear from her.

But I do have something to fear. No someone. Lux.

Slowly pulling my hand from the woman's firm hold, thoughts of father's warning about wolves and Lux stir through my mind.

"Well, he'll be disappointed because I won't be here," I begin, turning to make my way out of the door.

"Please, Winter, I don't think you understand," the woman pleads, quickly coming to my side, preventing my exit. "If you would but allow Lord Marchand to explain." Gesturing her hand for me to turn back to Lord Marchand, she casts a small smile.

Everything in me says I need to just leave and make my way to Rae, but I opt to indulge her request, for no other reason than the sweetness of her tone.

"My lord, I don't want to be rude or keep you from your evening, but I doubt there's really anything you could say—"

"Your father is wrong." Lord Marchand's matter-of-fact tone breaks through my protest.

"What?" My tone is brasher than it probably should be, but even if I am mad with my father, I don't want anyone casting blame on him.

"Let me rephrase that," he softens the tenor of his voice, raising his hands in caution. "What I mean to say is while there may be a Skull curse on Pack wolves, that curse doesn't apply to hybrids like Lux. Since he is part Altrinion and part Wolf, he is not subject to the Skull curse. The same way he has no need of submitting formally to a den or beholden to his wolfen form at a full moon, Lux has advantages other pack wolves do not have.

## Chapter Twenty-Three

And that one advantage keeps him at bay from such a curse."

My heartbeat slows and the frenzy running through me slows as Lord Marchand's words appear to be in slow motion.

*What we had was real?* I think to myself.

"Yes, Winter, everything you and Lux shared was in fact, very real. And he is on his way right now to prove it to not only you but to Lord Elysian as well. I only came ahead of him, with his sister-in-law, Abigail, to ensure you of that very fact."

Glancing up now through wet, thick lashes, I see Abigail looking at me with a doting grin as her hands remain clasped at her chin. She nods in agreement, still smiling. Looking at her, I recall Lux describing how much his brother loved her and how he never thought such a love could be his.

Could this be real? The man of my dreams. My fairytale? Is this really happening?

"He's coming here?"

"He's coming for you, Winter," Abigail sweetly says.

"And Lady Elysian, I have a feeling every happiness your heart desires will be yours. It's time for your happily ever after." Lord Marchand adds, donning a smile so confident, my knees do in fact buckle.

# Chapter Twenty-Four

*Winter*

"Rae!" I scream as I bolt through the front door.

Winded, I realize I've never ran so fast in my life. No sooner than Lord Marchand and Abigail were down the hall, I darted from the concierge desk, racing through the snow and plowing my way back into the house.

Knowing not only was I wrong about Lux, but he was still here and coming for me, gave me speed I never knew I had. While I hate to be the person to say, "I told you so," to my father, I am more than thankful to be right not only about my feelings for Lux, but his for me.

And with the way both Lord Marchand and Lux's sister-in-law, Abigail, were smiling, I have to believe Lux only spoke highly of me. Although it doesn't explain why he didn't come to tell me himself, I am just bubbling over to know I'd see him again.

"Rae!" I shout once more, still trying to catch my breath as I hold on to the banister at the base of the staircase.

"I'm right here, Win," Rae's quiet voice startles me from behind. Holding a teacup and saucer, she takes a sip before looking back up at me through wet lashes. Her puffy eyes give it all away. My poor cousin has been crying. "What are you doing back? I thought you were already *escorted* to the ball." Taking another sip, her clipped tone isn't lost on me.

She's mad at me.

"Oh, I'm sorry, Rae," I begin, wiping the one lone tear falling to her cheek. She turns her head away from me, batting her eyes as she stares up at the ceiling. Gently removing the cup from her hand and placing it on the small wooden table next to me, I throw her into my embrace. "I'm so sorry, Rae."

"I'm okay, really," she pulls herself from my hold, wiping her eyes with her wrist. "Besides, you and Kharon make sense. Uncle El is right, you need someone who can help you run things here. I'm happy for you, really, I am. I just need to—"

## Chapter Twenty-Four

"You don't need to do anything, Rae. Believe me when I say, there is no me and Kharon. I promise you," I add taking her hands in mine.

"But—but—I saw you two leave together, Win. You were arm in arm. You don't need to sugar coat it for me," Rae says, pulling her hands away.

Firming my grip, I gently tug her closer to me, leaning slightly to ensure our eyes lock. "Look Rae, the same way I know you don't take sugar in your tea, is the same way I know not to pull any wool over your eyes. That is not what I'm trying to do now, nor will I ever."

"What are you saying, Win?"

"I am saying, that yes, you did see me and Kharon leave the house together, but he only took me as far as the front door of the ballroom. And that's where I told him, I wasn't interested in him. Not now. Not ever."

"But—I thought—"

"You thought wrong."

"But Uncle El—"

"Look, Rae, I love my father, really I do. But I'll not now nor ever let him, or my mother completely run my life. Much less my heart. I'll always do what I can for the best of our family, but I cannot and will not allow anyone to dictate my heart. And I'll certainly not commit myself to someone I do not love—especially when the one I love is exactly who I believed him to be."

"What? Wait, are you saying—"

"Yes, Lux is the one for me. He's not who my father thinks he is. Even more, he's on his way to the ball now—"

"Oh my goodness, Win! I am so happy for you!" Rae says, tossing her arms around my neck.

"Thank you! Now, come on with me and get dressed! I'm not leaving you here to sulk another minute!" I squeal, pulling her arm to lead her up the stairs.

"Wait, Win, wait!" Rae grunts, resisting my pull. Folding her arms, she twists her mouth to one side, biting her bottom lip. "I'm happy for you, Win, I am, but I'm not stepping one foot in that ball. I don't want to spend the evening being your little tag-along cousin. Ross will be with Stephen, and you'll have Lux. And who will I have? No one. I'll just be the odd one out like always."

"*Like always*?" I repeat, worried. I've never seen Rae this bummed out. Between the three of us, she is normally our ray of light. Tonight, however, there's a dark cloud shrouding the light I normally see exuding from her. "Rae, I'm sorry. I don't mean to be insensitive. I had no idea you felt that way."

"It's nothing," she sputters, plopping on the stairs, pulling her curly hair to one side.

"Rae, please talk to me," I begin, squeezing next to her on the steps. Looking up at me through her thick, wet lashes, she forces a smile with a rosy,

## Chapter Twenty-Four

pink hue now blushing her cheeks. "This is about Kharon, isn't it? You really like him. Don't you?"

Nodding with her eyes only, she laughs slightly, pulling her knees to her chin. "Ugh, I must look like an idiot schoolgirl."

"No, Rae, you look like someone who's—dare I say, in love. After the day I had, I think I know what that looks like."

"Win, I know I'm always the cheerful one, and I'm sorry you have to see me like this, really I am."

"You don't have to apologize, Rae. It's not your job to keep us all happy and entertained. Besides, I'd rather understand just how you feel."

"I guess I suppress how I feel so much, masking it with laughter and jokes, it's hard admitting when I'm not happy."

"It's okay, Rae. I'm here. Share as much or as little as you'd like," I say, putting my arm around her.

"Okay," she begins, sitting up right, rubbing her tear-stained chin. "So, do you remember when I mentioned how I got trapped on the ski lift a few years back?"

"Yeah, during that crazy ice storm. That was right before I came back home when my father got sick."

"Yes, that," blowing out a heavy sigh, Rae pushes herself from the steps and begins pacing back and forth in front of me. "Okay, so I didn't get trapped on the ski lift alone. I was actually up there with Kharon."

My lips part slightly, but I work hard to keep my eyes from popping out of their sockets. I think I know where this is going. She pauses her pacing, staring at me. Nodding my head for her to continue, she circles the floor in front of me, twining her fingers together.

"Okay, well, nothing happened—nothing like that. But something did happen. We talked. We laughed. He kept me warm. He was sweet. And even though no kisses were shared it felt like *something* happened between us."

"Oh my goodness, Rae! I had no idea! Why didn't you tell me? Does Ross know?"

"I know, Win. I know. I didn't mean not to share it with you. But yes, Ross knows. He's my twin but even you know it's hard keeping anything from him."

While a part of me is frustrated Rae never told me, it's not as important as understanding how she feels now. "It's all right, Rae. I understand."

"No, you don't, Win. That moment on the ski lift with Kharon was something I wanted, really wanted to share with you, but I couldn't."

"Why? I would've understood, Rae. I told you, I'm not interested in Kharon Nyx."

"Well, I had every intention of telling you, but then Uncle El got sick. When you returned from

## Chapter Twenty-Four

school to tend to him and take care of things here, the time never felt right. But when Uncle El started getting better, it was like his first order of business was matching you with Kharon. Once he got his sails set in that direction, it seemed like whatever happened between me and Kharon on the ski lift was a distant memory. I mean granted I was hardly nineteen at the time, I assumed I was just crushing on an older guy and that Kharon couldn't possibly look at me that way. But there've been these moments, stolen moments, when his eyes lock with mine and I know—I just know it was more than a schoolgirl crush."

Gulping down the shock now knotted in my throat, I am taken aback by my cousin's reveal. "Wow, Rae, I had no idea."

"Look, I'm sorry to dish all this on you like this. It's just with everything going on—"

"It's all right, Rae. I appreciate you telling me. I just wish you didn't have to carry it around for so long." Standing up from the stairs, I take my cousin's hands once again, watching her eyes dance at the thought of Kharon. "All that matters to me is your heart, Rae. And I'll do whatever I can to make sure your heart is happy. Always. Please know that. You're more than a cousin to me. You're my sister and I love you!"

Pulling me in for a hug, Rae squeals, laughing and sobbing sweetly on my shoulder. "Thank you, Win! I love you too!"

# Chapter Twenty-Five

*Lux*

"Are you ready, brother?" Cedric asks, patting my shoulder hard as we stand on the outside of the ballroom entrance.

Taking a deep breath, I stare at the small, snow dusted pine trees with white lights adorned at the cobblestone walkway. With the iridescent lights twinkling like snowflakes accenting the doorway, I smile knowing this is all Winter's doing.

I can't help but be overwhelmed at the ambience she created just on the outside alone. Shiny, red oversized ornaments and stripped iron poles resembling candy canes illumine against the white brick building, making it look like Santa's workshop without the toys.

It's almost as breathtaking as Winter.

Almost.

"Ready," I mutter, practically breathless.

A myriad of thoughts waft through my mind and I wonder whether I'll be able to pull this off. What if I've already lost any chance to be with Winter? What if her father has painted me poorly? What if she decided to be with Kharon after all? What if the Changelings were right?

"Lux," Cedric's call of my name is hard like a whip, lashing me out of my brooding. "You've got this. Now, go get your bride." Cracking a small smile, I see the same pride within my brother I've seen more than once today.

My bride. Just the thought of making Winter my bride, flutters through my heart, slightly stiffening parts of me I now know only belong to her.

*Soon.* I say to my wolf with a low growl. He seems just as eager as I am.

"Ah, there he is!" My brother proudly exclaims, patting my back once more. "Steady yourself."

"I'm good, just eager is all," I answer as my chest heaves up and down. Thoughts of Winter swarm my thoughts and a deep rumble roars through my chest as I take heavy steps down the snow dusted walkway.

## Chapter Twenty-Five

Behind me, I hear Cedric whistle to the Guard as everyone shuffles behind him for instructions. "Okay, Dranoel, you and the rest of the Guard keep that with you. You can haul it around the back side of the building, and you'll get the signal from me when it's safe to bring it all in." My brother is at my side before I can open the door. "Please, Lux, allow me," Cedric says with a warm smile as he holds the door wide for me.

A brief wink is all I offer as I make my way inside. Once more, I am overcome by the wondrous sight before me. Lined along the wall, wearing white ribbed shirts with black bow ties, and cummerbunds are greeters holding small white boxes with red ribbons.

Making our way down the hall, one greeter steps out offering a gift box.

I don't have time for this.

"Please take one, sir," a young girl with a quivering voice says from behind a small desk.

"I'm sure Winter would want you to take one," Cedric whispers in my ear, feigning a tight smile back at the young girl.

A low growl is all I have to give in response as I look over my shoulder at my brother, annoyed. I don't want anything or anyone else stopping me from getting to Winter.

"We'll take two," Cedric offers his hand as he circles in front of me. The greeters hand the small boxes to Cedric, and he shoves one into my ribcage. "Here you go, brother. Now you see, that wasn't too hard," he sneers as I snarl while cupping the box under my arm.

"Great! Lady Winter has planned a nice tree trimming ceremony at the end of the ball. You'll use these at that time." Hearing Winter's plans, gives this gift box purpose. "Do you have anything you need to check?" the young girl asks, tousling her blonde hair to her side. Her bright smile tells me she's won over by my brother's charms. Although he's older than me by almost a century, his vampirism makes him appear a lot younger. I've grown accustomed to young women practically throwing themselves at Cedric when they spy his boyish face, but they wouldn't stand a chance. Abigail is his entire world.

I can relate.

"No, thank you. We're fine. Is the ballroom this way?" I ask softly, smiling as I step in front of my brother to take her attention from Cedric. A bashful smile crosses her face as I do, and she points us down the hall toward the ballroom.

"Ah, so you can be civil?" Cedric goads, leaning into me with his elbow as we saunter past the long line of greeters. Sighing, I shake my head, more frustrated by how long this corridor seems than my brother's teasing.

I am more than thankful when we reach the

## Chapter Twenty-Five

end of the hall as two doors open revealing a massive and stately ballroom.

The doors open as if the attendants on the other side anticipated our arrival. Smiling faces, both mortal and supernatural greet us as we make our way inside. I am surprised the ballroom seems bigger than I imagined. While the manor itself is sizeable, judging by the narrow corridor we took to get here, the grandeur of it all is unexpected.

With a massive sixteen-foot Christmas tree postured in the center of the room creating a circular effect, no doubt purposed to keep everyone engaged, I scan around the sizeable pine looking for the one person I want to see.

Winter.

Where is she?

"Do you see her?" Cedric whispers over my shoulder as he too looks through the crowd.

"No," I grumble, walking quickly by both familiar and unfamiliar faces seeking a casual chat. Knowing some mortals in the Regency are accustomed to an occasional fling with a supernatural regent, I allow no small talk or smiles that would give off the wrong idea.

I am not interested.

*All I want is Winter.*

Despite his vampiric speed, my brother works hard to keep up with my pace. No doubt he's stalling, knowing Lord Marchand frowns on us using our abilities in front of the mortals. I've never understood the reasoning behind hiding who we are in front of mortals in the Regency. They know who and what we are. Tonight, I could care less about proper protocol. The only thing I care about is finding Winter.

"Over there," Cedric, pulls my arm back hard as we circle the oversized Christmas tree. "There's Lord Marchand and Abigail. They're with Lord Elysian and his family now. I'm sure Winter can't be far."

No sooner than my brother's words left his mouth, I found myself now standing in between Lord Marchand and my sister-in-law. Dalcour frowns slightly as I do, likely annoyed I used my wolfen speed. Thankfully, Abigail's bright smile at my arrival helps me not feel like a total idiot.

"What is he doing here!" Lord Elysian shouts, pointing his cane at me.

His words barely upset me, but when I see Kharon come to Elysian's side from behind, a low growl blares through me. "Let me get security!" Kharon exclaims, pulling out his phone.

"Steady, Lux, steady," both Cedric and Abigail whisper in unison. Although their tones are too low for humans to detect, the calmness of their voices is enough to temper my mood.

Keeping my eyes set on Winter's father, and

## Chapter Twenty-Five

away from Kharon, I work hard to remember why I am here. I'll not allow Kharon Nyx to ruin this.

"Hello, Lord Elysian." I stammer my words, sounding less refined than I am. "It's good to see you again." I work hard to stretch a smile across my face, hopeful to douse the frustration I see brewing behind Winter's father's eyes.

"Ah-hem," Lord Marchand clears his throat, stepping in between me and Elysian. Holding his cane by only two fingers, Dalcour lowers Elysian's cane back to the ground, offering a gentle smile. "If you would only allow Master Decanter to apologize for his behavior earlier, I'm sure you two can come to some concession of sorts."

Apologize? For what? I have absolutely nothing to apologize for! What is Dalcour thinking? That is not why I came here. I came here for Winter and no one else. Everyone else can go to—

*You have to be willing to lay it all on the line for her.*

Memories of Cedric's words from before bridle my tongue and my love for Winter lassos my heart.

"Yes, my lord," I begin, stepping forward, meeting Lord Elysian's watchful glare. "I do want to apologize for my behavior. I had no right to speak to you as I did. For that, I am sorry."

Annoyed, Kharon blows out a sigh. "Please, my lord, do not let this wolf come here and—"

To my surprise, Lord Elysian interrupts Kharon's appeal, now moving his cane in front of Kharon. Winter's father's posture softens, and the tight scowl etched on his face recedes. "I accept your apology. But you must understand as a father I cannot allow my daughter to align herself with a pack wolf. Especially one whose only intent is to propagate his—"

"Now wait a minute," Cedric grits through his teeth as he jumps in front of Abigail, coming to my side. Watching my brother's fangs protrude, I am instantly reminded I'm not the only one in the family with a temper. Abigail grabs Cedric at his wrists, shaking her head in caution.

"No, brother, it's quite all right," I say, inching closer to Lord Elysian.

"Calm down, dear," a lovely woman, I presume is Winter's mother places her arms around Lord Elysian's waist and smiles back at me.

"Yes, Uncle El, you should at least hear Master Decanter out," Winter's cousin, Ross, chimes in, winking at me, adding an affirming smirk as he pulls his partner in close to his side. Briefly smiling in return, I am happy to see Ross is doing much better than before. I'm sure the brawny lumberjack at his side has something to do with that.

"Hold on," Lord Elysian begins, tilting his head to one side, narrowing his eyes, confused. "Did

## Chapter Twenty-Five

this one just call you brother?" Pointing at Cedric, Lord Elysian turns his gaze between us. "How is that possible? You are a wolf and he's an Altrinion-Vampire. This doesn't make any sense."

Cedric and I share a laugh, looking at one another. Abigail joins in as our joint laughter turns more heads in our direction. Lord Marchand smiles broad and places his hand on Lord Elysian's shoulder.

"Yes, yes, Lord Elysian, I'm afraid our world isn't as black and white as you may think," Dalcour replies.

"I don't understand. Will someone explain this?"

"I think I can explain it, father."

I would know that sweet voice anywhere.

Winter!

Now standing at the top step of a side entrance, my jaw drops looking at the most beautiful creature I've ever seen. Adorned in a gown the color of champagne, I want to drink up the entirety of Winter Elysian. Her shimmering cocoa-dusted skin shines beneath the twinkling lights as she strolls down the steps and it's taking everything in me not to scoop her in my arms and take her far away from here.

Offering her sweet smile, her pouty, raspberry coated lips look inviting, and a shiver shoots up my spine, aching to lock her lips with mine. But it's the way she looks at me as though I were the only man in the room that has my heart racing.

Before I can even ponder my motion, I am at the base of the staircase, offering my hand to Winter, helping her to the floor. I hardly notice the petite and pretty young woman trailing Winter, but seeing Winter turn her eyes back up the steps, I assume this is her cousin, Rae, and I aid her down the steps as well.

"You're here," Winter whispers, her eyes wide with surprise, fluttering her full, thick lashes.

"Where else would I be?" Lifting her hand to my lips, I smile. I couldn't resist at least one kiss.

## Chapter Twenty-Six

*Winter*

Today I've seen Lux naked, in lumberyard wear, and now standing before me looking dashingly handsome in a dark brown fitted tux accentuating every detail of his sculpted perfection.

*This man is fine!*

With his clean-shaven mustache and the way his wavy, asymmetrical locks hang above his golden and brown almond-shaped eyes, I can't help but be lost in the lure of Luxor Decanter. It's as if we are the only two in this entire ballroom.

But it's the grumbly faux cough of my father that brings me back to the moment. "Win?" My

*One Winters Kiss*

father begins, making his way toward me and Lux at the base of the stairs.

The rest of my family are on his heels with Ross beaming from ear to ear as his eyes dance between me and Lux. Covering his mouth and leaning into Stephen's side, Ross' excitement mirrors the giddy feeling swelling inside me as my hand deepens into Lux's grip.

"Darling," my mother interjects, rubbing my father's shoulders, likely attempting to douse his ire. "You look lovely tonight. We thought you and Rae were staying in. What changed?"

"Yes, what changed?" Father narrows his eyes at me, but I can tell he's not as upset as before.

"Well, I'll tell you what changed but first I think you should give Lux a chance to answer your question," I say, smiling up at Lux, noticing how he hasn't taken his eyes off me since he first took my hand.

"What? What does that have to do with anything—" Kharon stammers through the huddle my family has made around me and Lux.

"I'll hear him," my father huffs over his shoulder back at Kharon, raising his hand in caution. Kharon's face grimaces and he moves to take another step forward, but Lord Marchand and another man who slightly resembles Lux, firm their hands on his shoulders. Stretching his hand toward Lux, my father continues, "Yes, young man, do tell."

## Chapter Twenty-Six

"Yes, my lord," Lux answers, lowering his eyes almost dutifully toward my father. That'll surely earn him a few brownie points. "As you just heard, Cedric here is my brother. And while yes, he is vampire, he also Altrinion. As am I. Our father was a full blood Altrinion like Lord Marchand, and our mother, a full blood alpha wolf. Making us hybrids."

Gasps erupt among those eavesdropping nearby and Lux takes a moment to gaze around, smiling as though he were thankful for an audience. Slowly unlocking our clasped hands, he presses in the middle of the throng surrounding us, gesturing for the man, I now presume to be his brother to his side.

My eyes flit over to the bright smile and dancing eyes sweetly framing Abigail's face and my heart patters to see the admiration she has for her husband. She has every right to be proud. He is handsome. Although his features resemble Lux, his more youthful, dewy, butterscotch hued skin and dark crimson eyes embody the makings of an Altrinion-Vampire.

"I—I—don't understand," father says, with his hand on his chin. "I've never heard of such," he mumbles back to Lord Marchand.

"Ah yes," Lord Marchand replies as he saunters slowly next to my father. "Even more reason for young Lady Elysian to start her school."

"School?" My father exclaims, looking around the huddle and back at me. "What's this school I'm hearing of young lady?" Both confusion and frustration radiate through my father's eyes, and I wish this was something I could speak to him about without an audience. I really should've mentioned it long ago.

Before I can part my lips to speak, Lux makes his way back to my side, taking my hand in his. "I think what Lord Marchand is implying is there is much more to learn about the supernatural world. Perhaps, as head of the Regency, you'd allow Winter an opportunity to educate both mortals and supernaturals on such matters. At least that way, those in the Regency would understand how hybrid wolves like me can't fall to a Skull's curse, much less, put your daughter in danger of such a peril."

"Wait, wait, you mean to tell me that hybrids don't have to worry about being desolate, lone wolves?"

"Yes, my lord, that is exactly what my brother is saying," Cedric answers, his face glowing with pride. "As hybrids, we are able to choose our path, to remain Altrinion, or become wolf. Once we invoke either, we are set to live out our lives as such. However, as we are still at our core, Altrinion, a hybrid wolf outlives regular pack wolves.

"My word!" Mother sighs, with a hand at her chest. "Win, darling, did you know this all along?"

## Chapter Twenty-Six

"Well, Mother, yes and no. Yes, I knew Lux was a hybrid. But no, I didn't know what it meant in regard to the Skull curse. At least, not until Lord Marchand and Abigail told me earlier tonight."

"Yes, we wanted to clear that up so that Lux and Winter could be off to a good start and a clean state with you Lord Elysian," Lord Marchand adds, patting my father's shoulder.

"Besides, who doesn't love a good love story and a happily ever after!" Abigail chimes in, wearing a bright smile as she and Ross nod in agreement.

Stepping toward me, my father takes my free hand, turning my attention to him. He doesn't look at Lux as he does, staring at me as though no other voice mattered. "Is this true, Win? Are you in love with this man?" His voice is shaky, but his hold is firm as he locks his eyes with mine, ensuring I don't look elsewhere for answers.

Tears well in my eyes and for the first time I see my father's eyes glass too. "Yes father, I do love him." Squeezing his hand as I confess my love for Lux, my father's grip strengthens as if he didn't want to let go.

"And you love my daughter?" Father asks Lux without taking his eyes off me.

"Yes, my lord, I do," The last two words, *I do*, roar through Lux, making the four large crystal chandeliers in the ballroom shake.

"Well damn!" Ross shrieks, leaning into Stephen and fanning himself. Everyone around us echoes in laughter and I spy a rosy tint blush through Lux's cheeks as he bites his lips, slightly uncomfortable. Shaking his head as he looks at Ross, he laughs, hunching his shoulders as he returns his gaze back at me.

Sandwiching my palm between his hands, a small smile curves the corners of my father's mouth as he holds me tight in his grip. His eyes soften the frown lines he'd wore throughout the day, revealing the tender soul that makes me a true daddy's girl.

"Win, all I have ever wanted is your happiness, and if you've indeed found it with this young man, I will not stand in love's way."

"Oh daddy!" I squeal, tossing my arms around my father's neck as my eyes leak with joy. "Thank you!"

Kissing my cheek hard, my father pulls me into his side, turning us around to face Lux. "Young man, well who knows, if you're hanging with this one, you're probably older than me," father laughs, pointing his cane toward Lord Marchand. "As long as you promise to care for my daughter and treat her with nothing than the very best, you'll never have to worry about this old man interfering any further." Offering his hand to Lux with a smile that now reaches his eyes, I notice

## Chapter Twenty-Six

everyone is now either sniffling with joy or holding their breath—like my mother.

"Lord Elysian, I promise you I'll love Winter with my whole life. She shall never have a need and I swear to live faithfully for as long as I walk this earth." Shaking my father's hand, Lux smiles and I see his sun-spun eyes flash with gold.

My father backs up and Lux steps beside me and my mother comes closer, standing just at father's rear. "You did good, dear," she says softly, kissing my father's cheek. Reaching over his shoulder, he takes her hand in his, giving her peck on her knuckles.

"Well, I think this calls for a toast!" Ross shouts, waving his arm to a waiter to bring us champagne.

"Wait a minute!" Kharon bursts through the center of our huddle. "This is not happening!"

Rae steps up next to me, casting me a wary look.

"Look my boy," father starts, "I know I gave you my blessing to pursue Win. That was my mistake. I did so without thinking of her needs. I understand how upsetting this must be for you but—"

"But nothing Elysian!" Kharon's face tightens. Lux's posture stiffens as he regards Kharon, and I hear a low snarl rumble through him. "You made an oath. And that oath must be fulfilled."

"Look Kharon," I jump in as I sense both my father and Lux ready to rip into Kharon. Glancing at both Ross and Stephen, both of them look like they're ready to assist. I need everyone to calm down. "It's like I told you earlier, I don't see you that way. I never have. But that doesn't mean there aren't those who see the real you." Winking at Rae, I pull her wrist, suggesting it's time for her to take her shot. Her face reddens as she shoots a bashful smile to Kharon. His eyes soften slightly as he regards her, but when a hiss and snarl echo through both Cedric and Lux, Kharon's face darkens.

"Oh, Elysian, Win, if only you understood what you've done. I wanted to do this the easy, less painful way but now you've forced my hand. And now Melchior will truly die!"

Watching the malevolent grin smeared across Kharon's face, the once jovial hope springing within me dries, descending to the ground like the last leaf I saw this morning.

# Chapter Twenty-Seven

*Lux*

Despite the blazing fire from the oversized hearth fireplace not far from where we stand, an icy chill whips through the room, freezing everyone still.

The cheery faces Winter and her family had only moments ago are now shadow cast, despondent, and dim. Even the merry sounds of Winter's cousin Ross are reduced to a deafening silence. But it is the look of both horror and rage I sense kindling behind Lord Elysian's eyes that also stokes a looming unease in Winter.

Still, I have just brokered peace between me and Elysian, and I'll not allow Kharon Nyx to ruin it. Not now.

Another growl churns through me, and I feel my muscles tense, my wolf beckoning his release.

"Melchior?" Lord Elysian calls back to Kharon.

"Kharon," Winter's mother speaks in a soft tone, likely hoping to douse her husband's anger. "Why would you say something like that. You of all people know our beloved Melchior is no longer with us. He died at sea."

"Yes, and you're the one who found his ship!" Ross adds with the tenor of his voice deepening as he and Stephen now flank Winter's parents' sides.

"Is this true?" Lord Marchand asks Kharon after a quick and wary glance at me and Cedric.

Whipping his head back to Dalcour, a thick, smoky haze, reminiscent of what we saw in the cave, hovers around him. "What does it matter to you Altrinion?" he roars back. "All anyone need know is if Winter Elysian isn't mine, her precious brother Melchior will face a fate far worse than death. His soul will be condemned to the fires of Sheol!"

Cries and squeals swirl throughout the ballroom as an ominous glower now forms on Kharon's face.

"Unless you want the same to be Winter's fate, give her to me, Elysian!" Kharon demands as the smoke surrounding him thickens, suffocating the air in the tight space where we all stand.

Keeping Winter just behind me with my hand locked around her wrist, everything in me is ready

## Chapter Twenty-Seven

to shift and tear his head from his body, but Dalcour shoots me a look of warning and I keep my wolf at bay.

"Kharon," Rae whispers his name. Quickly he turns to face her, and for a moment I watch his expression soften. Stepping toward him, her glittery blue gown illumines under the chandelier, brightening the darkness around him. The way their eyes lock isn't lost on me, Cedric, or Abigail, but Kharon doesn't allow whatever there is between him and Winter's cousin to hold him hostage.

A loud, wailing howl bellows through him as he moves away from Rae's tearful glare. "Now Elysian, give Winter to me. All she need do is but give her heart to me, love me, and your beloved Melchior will be free."

"Please tell us you didn't have anything to do with my brother. Kharon, don't say you—" Winter cries into Rae's shoulder. Everything in me wants to hold her, but that will come soon enough.

"Oh Kharon, what have you done?" Lord Elysian mumbles as he works hard to maintain himself.

"I'll tell you!" I shout, squaring myself in front of Kharon, keeping him away from Winter.

"You know nothing, little wolf!" Kharon snaps back.

"Oh we know plenty!" Cedric offers, after shoving his palm in mine. Winking at me, I drop my hands inside my trouser pockets, as my brother and I share a laugh.

"Yes, Mr. Nyx—if that's even your name," I start as Winter's father makes his way to my side, looking up at me with a dim glint of hope in his eyes. "I know what you've done. For ten years you've trapped the young Lord Elysian in your cave, frozen by a Changelings curse. Your barter for entering this earthbound plane from the dark Netherworld."

"Kharon, is this true?" Lord Elysian demands a response.

"The only thing you need to know is your beloved Melchior bound himself to me—not the other way around—when he sought out his riches. It was his greed alone that assured him to this fate. And the only thing that will free him is when Winter is mine."

"Winter will never be yours, you wretched fool!" I sneer, snarling as my muscles constrict under the thin weight of my tux. One more contortion and my wolf takes over.

Lifting himself just a few inches from the floor, my brother's crimson eyes flash as his fangs lengthens. "Not only will the lovely lady never take your bait, but the bait you think you hold is no longer your own!"

Pulling my hand out of my pocket, I hold Kharon's obol in the air as his eyes hollow in fear.

## Chapter Twenty-Seven

"How did you?" He sneers, the darkened mist around him fading.

"Oh my brother and I have long been known for a little slight of hand," Cedric teases, now twirling Lord Elysian's cane in his hand. Winter's mother and cousins gasp as Elysian reaches up and snatches his cane back from Cedric, annoyed. "My apologies, sir but I only did so to prove a point. This horrid wretch has deceived you and your family long enough!"

"Yes, Lord Elysian, not only has he escaped, unmerited, into an earthbound plane which is forbidden, but in doing so has put your son in peril, with hopes to do the same to your daughter." Dalcour comes to me and Cedric's side, giving Cedric a stern glare, likely unhappy with his showcase of power in front of mortals. Still, he ignores my brother's antics, keeping his sights on Winter's father.

"Did you do these things, Kharon?" The anger in Winter's voice is hard to miss as she pulls herself from my grip, making her way in front of me. Quickly wrapping my arms around her waist, I nestle her in my hold, ensuring no one can snatch her away.

"What does it matter? You all have already made your mind up about me!" Kharon bites back.

"Not all of us," Rae whispers back in a tone too low for mortal ears to detect. Abigail's face falls as she exchanges a brief worried look with Cedric but keeps her eyes on Rae.

"I allowed you in my home, around my family, gave you almost unlimited access to my business dealings and all this time your only goal was to betray me!" Lord Elysian yells back, tossing his cane to the ground, pressing closer to Kharon. Ross and Stephen hold him back as he does and Rae whimpers, leaning into her aunt's embrace.

"Not once did I seek to betray you. I only wanted to return your son to you. And the only way I could do so was through Winter. That I promise you!"

"I don't understand," Ross steps in front of his uncle. "What does any of this have to do with Winter? And why is Melchior your prisoner?"

Lowering his eyes, Kharon almost seems repentant. "I never said he was *my* prisoner."

"So you're just keeping my brother stowed away for your own depraved pleasure!" Winter's mood is fierce. Even if I weren't here, I have no doubt she can hold her own ground. Neither the cloud of smoke surrounding Kharon, nor the more gangly features now shaping his face strike fear in her. "I don't care what you want from me, you'll never get it!"

"Then your brother will be damned to an eternity in Sheol! That is a fate that your lupine mate, nor his vampire companions can cure."

## Chapter Twenty-Seven

Kharon replies as the cloud around him dissipates and his form becomes more decrepit.

"On the contrary," Dalcour counters as he paces in front of the crowd. "One thing about the Changelings, is that there is always a loophole—because they never quite tell the whole truth."

"What?" Kharon questions, now looking more elderly than Lord Elysian. Horrorstruck, the spectators around us, both mortal and supernatural, shriek at the sight before them. I take special notice that only Rae maintains her composure as she keeps her eyes fixed on him.

"You see—and yet another reason why Winter really needs to start this school—" Dalcour adds casually as if Kharon's deformity weren't happening before our very eyes. "The Changelings may have told you that because you were bound to the obol, any mortal holder of the obol is bound to you except they be saved by the blessed true love's kiss; they failed to mention one thing. You see, Kharon, it is not your kiss alone that can set the young Lord Elysian free. Is it, Lux?" Turning to me, Dalcour's calculating smirk is all the signal I need.

"No! It can't be!" Kharon gasps, staggering across the floor. Lord Marchand and Cedric step in front of him, preventing him from coming closer.

Taking Winter's chin in my hand, I turn her away from Kharon, smiling, hopeful to keep her eyes locked on me. "Winter Elysian, I love you," I confess, staring into her beautiful, yet bewildered gaze.

"I love you too, Lux, but—" Placing a finger on her full lips, I bid her quiet.

"But nothing, Winter, please keep your eyes on me," I whisper, watching the flash of gold of my eyes mirror in her own. Fluttering her gaze back to me, she smiles. "Now kiss me."

And kiss me she does.

# Chapter Twenty-Eight

*Winter*

*Now kiss me.*

How a man I only met today can command my lips to lock with his with just three words, I'll never understand. But my parents always told me comprehension was not a requisite of obedience. And the ways my body wants to obey every word of Lux Decanter has my passionate pixie leaping for joy.

Neither my pixie nor my lips care that I'm not only surrounded by a ballroom of both supernaturals and mortals but my entire family. As Lux tightens his hold on me as the lock and tether of our tongues swirl together, I have no doubt I'm detecting a tap of his stiffened member at my abdomen.

Keeping his hand along the small of my back, Lux slows our pacing, planting one last small kiss on my mouth, sealing my lips.

"My how I love you, woman," he croons in my ear, grunting, working hard to keep his composure. The way he deepens his gaze into me, everything in me wants to forget we still have the atrocities of Kharon to address. Still, I take a moment to appreciate the love I see radiating through Lux's eyes as he stares at me.

"My lords!" A loud shout from outside the terrace doors, yanks us back to the moment. Turning quickly, we see two men, dressed in black holding the French doors open. "It worked!" they scream in unison.

"And this ladies and gentlemen, is the power of true love's kiss!" Dalcour heaps a hearty laugh as he gestures hands toward the terrace.

Grumbles of concern echo through the ballroom, but I nearly faint when I watch my brother Melchior amble across the threshold. Lux steadies his arm around my waist as knees buckle at the sight of the miracle before me.

Ross and Rae wrap their arms around my mother as a waterfall of tears stream across their faces. Dropping his cane, my father straightens

## Chapter Twenty-Eight

his posture, willing himself toward Melchior's path. Melchior's footsteps are wobbly as he makes his way inside. Stephen quickly leaves Ross's side toward Melchior, putting his arm around his shoulder to aid him forward.

Taking no time to take my brother's shoulders in his grasp, my father looks Melchior up and down, his face full of awe. "My—my—son!" he cries. "My boy! My precious boy!"

"Dad—dad!" Melchior buries his head in my father's embrace, sobbing inconsolably into my father's chest. "I'm so sorry father. I never should've left. I'm so sorry!" His words are almost incoherent as he pounds his fists against my father's arms, desperation pouring out with each word.

"You're home now, my boy! And I'll never let you go again!" My father bellows, holding Melchior tight in his hold.

My vision is blurred as a stream of tears gush out. I could care less how the spillage is likely making a dark trail of mascara run down to my chin. All I want is to hug my big brother.

"Come beautiful, I'll take you to him," Gently, Lux's fingers wipe away my tears as he looks at me tenderly.

"You think you've won!" Kharon lashes out, the vehemence of his tone sullying our reunion. "Young Elysian has tampered with things he can't possibly understand! Before the end you'll beg for my help!" Pulling out the same black velvet box from earlier, he shakes out the contents, revealing shiny onyx crystals as they fall to the ground.

Rae presses forward but with sounds like fireworks, crackling about, Ross yanks her back. Cedric and Lord Marchand rush toward Kharon, but he stomps his feet hard into the black sand, disappearing into a dark cloud.

"Kharon! No!" Rae calls out, crumpling to her knees in shock. Ross wraps his arms around Rae as she bawls within his hold.

"Go look for him!" Lord Marchand orders the two men at the terrace door. Shutting the doors behind them, they immediately disappear into the night.

Lux hugs me tighter, pulling me away from Kharon's dark smoke. Yet, it clears quickly, and I see my father and brother on the other side, and I grab Lux's hand, tugging him toward my family.

Mother also makes her way to my side as we join my father and Melchior. Looking at Melchior, it's as if no time has passed. He looks just as youthful today as he did the last time I saw him. My brother was my age when he disappeared—or at least when we thought him dead.

Looking into his hazel eyes and creamy brown skin, he looks as if he's been well-preserved.

"Melchior?" I say, taking his face in my hand. Still wearing the black trousers and blue button-down shirt, he wore religiously before his departure, Melchior looks like he stepped right out of an old photograph.

"Little Win?" he gasps, looking at me in shock. "How is any of this possible? How long have I been asleep?"

"Ah, Young Lord Elysian," Lord Marchand begins, smiling as he walks away from the terrace toward us. "It's good to see you again. It has been too long. Over a decade, in fact."

'Ten years!" Melchior shrieks, patting himself, and turning to look into an adjacent mirror on the wall. "But I still look—"

"As handsome as ever," Mother adds, kissing his face and tossing her arms around him.

Walking to the staircase, Lord Marchand taps against a champagne glass, holding it up to get our attention. "Members of the Regency, both mortal and supernatural, tonight our eyes have witnessed the perils that can rise against us if we do not stand as a united front to ward against the perils and darkness, seeking to slink into our midst. Here and now, as your leader, I take full responsibility for not seeing to the matters of this Regency regularly. I assure you, that will never happen again. From this day forward I shall ensure the Guardians, with Luxor Decanter at the helm, see to the protection of your lands. Working alongside Lord Elysian, he will ensure each regent is kept both informed and safe—that is with Lord

Elysian's blessing." Extending his hand toward my father, Lord Marchand smiles as the room awaits my father's reply.

Still overtaken by my brother's return, my father remains speechless. A first.

Before I can reply, the sound of Melchior's voice makes my heart jump for joy. "If this be my father's will, I will stand at his side to see it done!" My brother pledges, as my father looks up at him with admiration.

Bellowing a hearty laugh, Lord Marchand clanks his glass once more as the server's hand give drinks to everyone in the ballroom. "Now let us raise our glasses high in thankfulness of the return of the beloved Young Lord Melchior's return!"

"Here-here!" Ross, Stephen, and Cedric shout back in unison as the room resounds with a gleeful cheer.

Instead of lifting a glass, Lux kisses the top of my head, confessing another sweet *I love you* and squeezing me at the waist, keeping me glued to his side. His hold is everything I need right now. Leaning into his embrace, my fingers graze the buttons along his chest, and I realize something, *this is my dream come true.*

# Chapter Twenty-Nine

*Lux*

The Elysians spend the remainder of the evening fussing over Melchior. Seating him at his father's place at the high table, nearly spoon-feeding him and attending to his every need. I'm more surprised it's Lord Elysian doing more of the doting than even his wife or Winter. Smiling, but still a bit disoriented from the evening's events, Melchior indulges his family's fawning.

Rae, however, stays noticeably quiet. While it's obvious she's happy for her cousin's safe, albeit magical, return, her constant and pensive gazing out of the window doesn't go unnoticed by me.

Although I am unsure whether Winter or even Ross sense her dissonance as Rae finds small ways to insert herself into her family's conversations along the way.

"Did they have any luck finding Nyx?" I ask Cedric when he returns from talking with Dranoel near the terrace. I am sure Dranoel came by to give my brother and Lord Marchand an update.

"Negative ghost rider," Cedric quickly answers, leaning into my shoulder. "But now isn't the time to worry about Nyx."

"How can I not? Neither Winter nor her family is safe as long as that filth walks about freely!" I grit through my teeth, keeping my voice low as to not cause a scene.

"Brother," Cedric begins, tightening his hold at my elbow. "There will always be some sort of threat—something to worry about. All you can do is enjoy whatever time you are given. Supernatural, mortal, or otherwise—we can ask no more."

"But—"

Lifting his hand with his eyes closed, Cedric turns his head away from me in protest. "But nothing! Now go, enjoy the evening! Dance with your mate!" Cedric pushes me and I snarl back but he bares his fangs, laughing.

Our jaunty, brotherly antics stir just enough attention for Winter to take notice as she looks at me from her place at her mother's side. Her nose

## Chapter Twenty-Nine

scrunches in the cutest way possible and she tilts her head, curious.

"Dance? Really, brother?" I hunch my shoulders, shaking my head.

"Yes, dance, little brother," Cedric answers, propping his arm on my shoulder. "In fact, I've already advised Abigail to ask the disk jockey to play a little ditty—something special, just for you and Winter." Looking at the DJ table, my sister-in-law waves at me smiling, giving me a thumbs up.

Huffing, I know there's no stopping this lovesick duo. Winter's eyes remain on me as I make my way to the table and I extend my hand toward her, "Excuse me, Lord Elysian and high table, if you would pardon the lady Winter for a dance?"

"Fancy!" Ross coos his teasing into Stephen's ear, chuckling as he stands to pull the chair out for Winter.

Lord Elysian smiles back at me, nodding in agreement as Winter stands from the table as Ross holds her hand as she walks down the steps off the riser. Melchior seems pleased as he regards his sister, giving me his wink of approval.

Taking her hand as she reaches the bottom, I hear a familiar piano beat pour through the sound system, and I smile. My brother knows how much I enjoy the music of Leslie Odom, Jr. Hearing *Winter Song* blare through the ballroom may be a little on the nose, but it's certainly fitting how I feel right now.

"May I have this dance?" I ask, kissing her wrist.

Winter pants as soon as my lips connect with her skin. I wish I was kissing other parts of her. But this will have to do for now.

"You don't even have to ask," she beams, her eyes already dancing.

Leading her to the center of the ballroom, our hands clasp together as I firm my hold gently at her back. It feels so good to hold her. She lets me lead our movement as our bodies sway and twirl under the snowflake lit chandeliers.

Time stands still as Winter nestles herself deeper into my hold and I see no one in this room but her. Her big bright eyes. Her soft curly black hair. Her perfectly pouty lips. Everything about Winter Elysian is pure paradise. Looking into her eyes, I know she is more than my love, she is my home.

There is no where I'd rather be.

Well, perhaps one other place. But that will come soon enough.

Tossing her arms around my neck, Winter chuckles, and I am thankful she's no longer covering her lovely smile. "What's so funny, beautiful?" I ask, but I am really just happy to see her smile.

## Chapter Twenty-Nine

"I just can't believe all of this is real. Us. Like this is happening. Really happening," she laughs once more.

"Believe it, Winter. You're stuck with me now," I say, nuzzling her nose. Winter giggles again, likely tickled. Smiling at her, I do it again. It's a wolf mating gesture. An intimate moment for my wolf to mark my scent on her. Not quite the marking I'll do when I imprint on her when we make love for the first time, but this marking tells any wolf or supernatural creature that Winter is indeed mine.

All mine.

While I plan on explaining all of this to her soon, after the day we've had, I'm not taking any more risks.

"Looks like we've got company," Winter adds when we notice Ross and Stephen make their way onto the dance floor. Cedric and Abigail aren't far behind. From there, it doesn't take long for others to join in.

The song changes to Odom's Stronger Magic, and I change up our rhythm, fusing more jazzy steps to our foxtrot. While I am more than happy to carry the weight of leading our movements, I am surprised how Winter holds her own. The woman has moves!

There have been few times I've been at ease around humans, and more often than not, dancing has been the common denominator. My brother knows this—hence his pushing me out onto the dancefloor.

"Oh, Winter I love the way you move," I croon at her ear.

With a sexy smirk, she only gives me a seductive stare in return, leaning back as I dip her low. "Oh, just wait until I'm back on my throne, I've got moves only meant for you." Tracing her fingers along my jawline, both her touch and her words send a reaction straight to my manhood.

"You've got that right, sweetness, everything that is you—is all mine," I reply, lifting her back up to meet the desire in my eyes. Smirking once more, I see the makings of a little vixen laced within her smile.

"And you're mine, Lux Decanter," she answers, lowering my head to her lips.

If she were my wife nothing would stop me from yanking her from this place and into our bed. My wolf forces a sensual yelp at her kiss, and I now know without a doubt my wolf has claimed Winter as an acceptable mate.

But I don't have long to revel in thoughts of us making love before I hear a faux cough behind me and a light tapping of my shoulder.

"Father!" Winter nervously exclaims. Although to onlookers we appear to just be standing here, it's clear to both me and Winter—*we were indeed eye fuc*— "Yes, father, mother—oh, and Melchior."

## Chapter Twenty-Nine

Winter's jumpy posture doesn't go unnoticed as her brother gives her a knowing glance and her mother looks up at the ceiling, turning her eyes as not to cause Winter undue shame.

Thankfully, Lord Elysian seems oblivious to our shared cavorting; and for that I am thankful.

"Lux, I can't thank you enough for everything you and yours did for me and my family," Elysian states, reaching out to shake my hand.

Gripping his palm in mine, I am shocked at his firm hold and sturdy shake. "I am just glad I could help, my lord. I'd do anything for Winter and your family."

"That's good to hear," he begins, and I watch him look over his shoulder at his wife, and I know he has a favor to ask. Little does he know, whatever he asks of me for Winter's sake, I'll do it. "Because I have to ask you something."

"Mom, Dad?" The worry in Winter's voice is clear. She never casually addresses her parents, but even she is picking up on something going on. I nod for Lord Elysian to continue as Winter's eyes widen with concern.

"Well, I can tell you are a good man, and I know you only want the best for my daughter. That is why I know I can ask this of you. While you've yet to make a formal proposal for Winter's hand, I ask that you once you do, you two delay the actual ceremonies a bit. At least for a little while. I've just gotten my family back and I can't gain one child, only to lose another. Not yet. So what do you say, my boy? Can I count on you to hold off on the nuptials?"

It's as every bit of oxygen is sucked from my lungs at once. Just the thought of not making Winter mine is more suffocating than both my time in the well and Kharon's dark smoke combined. *Damn!*

# Chapter Thirty

## *Winter*

"Father, no!" I cry out, shuttering the whimsical merriment of the ballroom. Lux takes my arm, calling my name, but his words are muted by the brazen request of my father.

"Win, dear, just hear your father out," my mom whispers, looking around the room, embarrassment blushing red beneath her cocoa covered cheeks.

"I thought you two were finally respecting my decisions—respecting me as an adult! But here you are trying to control me yet again!"

"Baby, let's just hear your father out." Despite his gentle tone, Lux's words break into my rant as his warm hand locks with mine, soothing the gnawing ache within me.

"Fine, let's hear it!" As annoyed as I am, I can't help wondering if seeing the intensity between me and Lux on the dancefloor was too much. Even so, the thought of my father literally cock-blocking me is frustrating.

"Look, Win, it's clear to me that you and Lux are eager to start a life together and I want that for you. I've always only wanted nothing but your happiness. You know this," my father starts, lifting my chin, forcing me out of my sulking. "But your brother just returned. I only want you to take some time to help him adjust—catch him up on what he's missed. Over the last few years you've been the glue to keep this estate operating as smoothly as it has. I can't expect Melchior to just pick up where he left off."

"Sis, no worries," Melchior pops in between me and my father. "I've always been a quick learner. Like I told father, I'm sure I'll be fine." My brother casts a reassuring smile at me that tugs my heart strings.

Maybe I could slow it down a bit. Lux and I share a quick glance, likely thinking the same thing.

"Quick learner, eh," Ross chimes in. "Yeah, because you're quite capable of posting reels on the Gram and managing ad posts for the Book."

## Chapter Thirty

Melchior looks back at Ross confused. Although Facebook was around before Melchior disappeared, he never took to it. And now there are even more social media tools to learn. Not to mention all of the new things we've added to both the pine fields and the estate.

Looking up at Lux, I know the challenge this presents for both of us. But I can see my heart strings aren't the only ones pulled. Kissing my forehead, Lux smiles, strumming his hand along my face, assuring me everything will be okay.

"Lord Elysian, I can appreciate your need to want to ensure to the matters of your estate and bond your family together. That said, Winter will also be my family and as her husband, I too, will look out for her interests as well."

"Wait, Lux—" I pull at his arm as I see my father's face tightening. Lux offers his dashing smile at me, and I worry whether his charms are enough to sway my father.

"I'm listening," Father says, lifting his brow and leaning into his cane.

"If Winter agrees to staying on and not only working with the Young Lord Elysian, as well as sharing in a reunion of sorts with your family, I only ask that she also be given an opportunity to complete the last semester of her graduate degree."

Stunned, both Ross and I cover our mouths in shock, fully surprised by Lux's counteroffer.

"It's important to me that Winter takes time to do the things she not only loves to do, but wants to try," Lux continues as he saunters between us.

Abigail, Cedric, and even Lord Marchand rejoin our huddle. Smiling at me, Abigail wraps her arm around me, allowing our heads to lean into one another. For as affectionate as Lux's sister-in-law is, it hardly seems like we just met today.

"I see," my father says, twisting his mouth, contemplating. "And so are you talking about her starting this school I keep hearing you reference?"

"Well, not only the school, my lord, but according to Winter, she's barely left this island. I think it would be good for her to see the world. Explore new things—"

"Learn to ice skate!" Ross shouts quickly before cupping his hand. Shoving him in his side, I shake my head. "I mean come on, Win, it's ridiculous that you never learned to skate. I mean we live in the North Pole!"

"Ross, this is hardly the North Pole!" I playfully banter, hitting his shoulder.

"Wait a minute! My sister hasn't learned to skate?" Melchior chimes in, laughing with Ross. "Well, we can't have that!" High-fiving Ross, the two continue their amusement at my expense, and it reminds me of my childhood.

Lux looks at me, and the care I see in his eyes, swells me with happiness. Still, I have questions. "Lux, what about us?" I ask.

## Chapter Thirty

"It doesn't change anything, Winter. It just means we'll have to delay our nuptials a tad."

"You mean until the semester is over? How long?"

"However long you need, baby," Lux says, taking my hand in his. "But your father is right, your family needs you."

"But you are my family, Lux," I protest. "You all are." Looking over my shoulder at Abigail and Cedric, both smile at me, hugging one another tighter. Lux's eyes glass at my sentiment, and I realize I've found another route to his heart. His family.

I am not surprised. Because that's how I feel for my family as well.

"Hold on," Ross begins, lifting a cautionary finger. Everyone rolls their eyes, but I soon notice I don't see Rae and I am sure Ross will question his twin's whereabouts. "Lux riddle me this, if you're a wolf—an Altrinion Hybrid or whatever—what does this mean for Win? I mean she's mortal. Can she be with a wolf?" Pounding his hand back and forth, everyone sighs at his crass. "I mean don't you all act like you weren't wondering the same thing!"

"Oh Ross, really you can be so tactless!" My mother chides, swatting his hand in motion.

Lux appears more uncomfortable than anything, but he covers his smile and leans into me. "Is your cousin always like this?"

"Always," I nod back.

Lux heaves a heap of air, blowing it out as he fixes his gaze on my father. "My lord, do you find my terms amenable?" I am thankful Lux turns his attention away from Ross's lack of diplomacy.

Distracted, my mother taps my father's shoulder, bringing him back to the moment. "Dear, are you fine with what Lux said?"

"Oh, um—that—well, as long as Winter is good with it, I am. But Ross does bring up a good point. Well, not so much the mating part—I really don't want to know the specifics of that. But as an Altrinion, if you live as long as Lord Marchand, what does that mean for your relationship with my daughter?"

Crap! Leave it up to my father to check all the boxes. It is a good question. Will I just die, leaving Lux to move on to his next wife? How many times has he done this? *Maybe we do need to take it slow.*

"Ah-hem," Lord Marchand begins, with a wink at me. "Perhaps I can help ease your angst, Young Lady Winter." Darn it. I forgot Altrinions can read minds. I wonder if Lux can read my mind. "First, let me say, how happy I am for both you and Lux. And no, wolves can't read minds, but their intuition and sensory awareness is higher than any other," he whispers in my ear, now standing next to me. Lux glances at Dalcour briefly before

*Chapter Thirty*

smiling down at me, nodding in agreement. "But to answer your question Lord Elysian, once Lux and Winter mate, she takes on the magic that makes him supernatural. And before you ask, no, she doesn't become a wolf, but his longevity of life will be hers as will his speed and some of his strength become her own. As the Good Book says, the two shall indeed become one."

Walking toward us, my father takes both mine and Lux's hand. "Lux, I am honored to give you my blessing. That is, my boy, are you now ready to propose to my daughter?"

Without hesitation, Lux shoots out one word, destined to bind us as one. "Yes." The room oozes in anticipation as Lux holds out my hand and leads us into the center of the of the ballroom in front of the Christmas tree. "If we've learned nothing else tonight, we've learned that both the mortal and supernatural world can live together in harmony. We've proved that tonight," Lux says, sharing a nod of agreement with both my father and Lord Marchand. Signaling Cedric and Abigail to our sides, Lux continues, "Now with the gifts each of you were given at your arrival I ask that you come and place your ornaments on the tree, leaving your gift boxes at the base of the tree."

Surprise overtakes me at his gesture, and I can't help wondering how Lux knew this is what I envisioned. Mortals, vampires, and wolves are all adorning the massive tree with their gifts. A colorful array of silver, red, and gold sparkle as everyone places their ornaments on the Christmas tree, making my heart melt with joy.

Taking my hand, Lux helps me atop a small silver bench as Cedric and Abigail grip the railing. I don't have a chance to ask what he's doing before they lift us to the top of the tree. Holding the silver snowflake I made from the gift box, my heart flutters.

"Winter Elysian," Lux begins with a smile that melts my heart in two. "Until I met you, I never believed in happily ever after. I never truly understood love. But it only took one chance encounter to change my world forever. And that world starts with you. Would you please do me the honor and become my wife?"

"Yes, Lux, yes!" My tearful reply is met with a kiss from Lux Decanter that beats out not only all the book boyfriends ever written but all the would-be Prince Charming's of the storybook legend.

Only hours ago, I thought fairytales were merely figments of my imagination. But with one kiss, I now know dreams can come true.

*"I love you,"* both Lux and I declare in a sweet whisper as we slowly tear away from our kiss. Together, we lift the snowflake and place it at the top of the tree. As we do, someone below lights the tree and we share in another brief kiss as the

*Chapter Thirty*

room erupts in clamors of claps, shouts and whistles.

"To the happy couple!" Ross shouts as Cedric and Abigail lower us back to the floor and everyone raises their glasses in toast.

Nestling myself deeper into Lux's hold, I wish I could freeze this moment in time. Then I realize, I don't have to. This is the beginning of our forever.

# Chapter Thirty-One

*LUX*

*One Year Later*

This is the day I've waited for since the day I met Winter Elysian. The day when I make her my wife.

The last year with Winter has been an adventure. I made my first quest a lesson in ice-skating. Her father had kept her too busy over the years to bother with such trivial matters as he once said. That's why on Christmas morning, or rather Winter's birthday, I took her to the local rink. Her entire family came as well. Ross supplied the hot chocolate, while her mother brought along Winter's favorite, blueberry grunts for us all to share.

*One Winters Kiss*

I was happy to see Winter take to skating relatively easy. She seems to have a knack for excelling in just about everything she puts her mind to. So to commemorate the occasion, I gave her an ice globe from the gift shop. I told her we'd collect memorabilia of our ventures. She seemed to really like that idea.

The first few months were spent with Winter knee-deep in school to complete her master's and graduating. A good portion of that time she also spent reconnecting with her family and teaching Melchior the ropes.

It turns out Elysian did indeed raise Winter as he did his son. The two are certainly two sides of the same coin. Which is a good thing because their likeness aided Melchior in picking up everything rather quickly. Although Winter does worry her brother suffers from night terrors due to being trapped under a Changeling's influence for so long. Melchior does his best to shrug it off, hopeful not to cause his family much concern.

While Ross remains—well—Ross, a feisty romantic who seems like he and Stephen are in it for the long haul, Rae is a bit distant. She hasn't been the same since Melchior returned. Winter believes Rae is secretly seeing Kharon. Of that I can confirm since she often reeks of his deathly stench. Both Ross and Winter are worried about her but fear confronting her will make matters worse.

## Chapter Thirty-One

Winter, however, was more than ready to confront Kharon herself. But when I informed her how the Changelings work, and that their witchcraft was probably as much as a trick to Kharon as they were to Melchior, she relented. I think she figured if I no longer saw a need to tear him in two, she could let it go.

At least for now.

Surprisingly, Lord Elysian appears more lively. I am certain having his son back has renewed him in ways he never thought possible. Even more, the two of us have gotten close. While at times he wants to remind everyone he is indeed the patriarch, he never fails to esteem me as Winter's mate.

For that alone I am thankful.

As a matter of fact, we're working on a joint surprise as a wedding gift to Winter. Transforming the lumberyard cabin into our first home. I thought it appropriate since it is the place where we shared our first kiss.

Thankfully, Winter has been so busy working with Abigail, Cedric, and Trieu on developing plans for starting a school next season, that she's had no time to visit the lumberyard. Mostly, I think she fears she'll come upon Stephen and Ross, but she has no idea that they spend most of their time at Stephen's place, knowing our plans for our new home.

We've added an addition to it and expanded the kitchen. It's still the cozy place where we first fell in love but will work fine when we add to our family. And I have every intent on starting on that family tonight.

"Still can't tie a tie, huh brother?" Cedric teases, suddenly appearing at my side, jolting me from my musing. "Turn around, let your big brother help you."

Sighing, still annoyed how at almost three-hundred years, I am still referred to as *little brother*. "I can tie it, I'm just fumbling. My mind is all over the place."

"Well, settle yourself brother. In just a little while you'll join with your mate."

"You don't think I'm rushing it, do you? Is it too soon? Rushing my wolf could cause the mating to stall and then—"

"Calm yourself, Lux," Cedric says, taking my chin in his hand. "You've been a dutiful mate. And so has Winter. It's been almost a year to the day. And with the full moon in view, I have no doubt that your mating will go as planned. But that's not what you're worried about, is it?"

Pausing, we both stare at one another, looking at ourselves in the mirror. "There's been so much going on. I mean even I thought it would be a good thing when Lord Marchand fell in love with—"

"Please don't bring it up! Ever since he fell for Damina his life has been one big wrecking ball—

## Chapter Thirty-One

and the Prime Alpha Jackson Nashoba makes three! I wouldn't want to be anywhere near that mess."

"Yeah, but—"

"But nothing, brother. If watching the love triangle of Dalcour, Damina, and Jackson could teach you anything, it should teach you never to take the one you're with for granted. And that's why you're here, right now, ready to marry the woman you love."

Thinking of my brother's words, it has been difficult to watch Dalcour's romance play out. It's no secret he always idolized what Cedric and Abigail shared. Even after I proposed to Winter, the gleam in his eye told me, that he even wished for what Winter and I shared. Perhaps he wanted it so much he pushed things too fast. I, on the other hand, am the complete opposite.

I was looking for anything but love. *And then I found Winter.* The love of my life.

Nudging my arm, I can see Cedric is desperate to change the subject. "Oh what's this I hear you had Abigail go purchase some expensive crown? I've never heard of such for a wolf wedding or necessary in mating rituals. Do you need me to do something with it? Or is Winter wearing it during the ceremony?"

My heart flutters as I think of the platinum gold crown with chocolate diamonds, I asked my sister-in-law to pick up for me. We'd been so deep in

Dalcour's drama happening in New Orleans, I almost forgot my promise to my bride. That flutter goes straight to the seat of my pants and I'm thankful my brother is too busy sating his thirst to notice.

Licking my lips, the thought of being with my soon-to-be wife, sends my hormones into overdrive. "No, Cedric, she's not wearing it during the ceremony. At least not any ceremony you'll witness."

In fact, no one but my wolf is privy to the plans I have for the queen who wears my crown tonight. After all the teasing Winter has put me through during our long engagement, I plan on seeing my Winter Queen shine brighter than any tree topper or Christmas star.

And she'll shine bright just for me.

# Chapter Thirty-Two

## *Winter*

The last few months have been the longest I'd been without Lux. While I'm sure he regrets taking me back to Louisiana, a place he's called home for well over one hundred years, it was great seeing a part of the United States I'd only seen on television.

I kept picturing it like a mix of *Interview with a Vampire* and *True Blood*.

Boy was I wrong!

Well, not entirely. Before I could see too much, Lux had Abigail rush me back home. As ranking leaders of the Guard both Cedric and Lux will stay on until things got under control. Apparently,

Lord Marchand took a monstrous turn for the worse.

And although Cedric claimed it was typical of Altrinion Vampires like Marchand; especially since he was a rare breed. A Fated Mate; he and his beloved are of the few who are destined for one another. A fate with a pull so strong that things go awry. Lux didn't want to take any risks with me when things went haywire.

The whole ordeal took months to reconcile, and it's actually still in a bit of limbo even now. But when I found Lux seated in the foyer of the manor when I came down for breakfast this morning, the look in his eyes told me he wouldn't wait another day to see us married.

Apparently, he'd been working with my parents to ensure every detail. If I had to guess, I'm sure both Ross and Rae have been involved as well.

Although I was eager to be with Lux since the day we met, I am glad we took this time together. We've learned so much about one another. We've disagreed and downright argued. Sometimes over the silliest things like what tastes better—turkey burgers or beef burgers. Of course he was on the side of beef, insisting our children will only eat food as intended. In his words, "turkeys are served with gravy and mashed potatoes—not on buns with cheese!" I'm not sure why it angered me so much, but it did.

## Chapter Thirty-Two

But after a few kisses, he began to see things my way.

As a matter of fact, I'm learning even more *creative* ways to get him to see things my way. Not that I want to make a habit of using sex as a tool to manipulate my husband, it is good to know I can at least encourage him a little.

Lux has maintained to keep me a virgin until our wedding night, spouting the same wolf ritual stuff since the first day, but a girl has needs. Luckily for me, I've coaxed him into assuaging my needs on more than one occasion.

Pulling up my garter and hose now, I recall a time we were in New York. We had just seen Hamilton and Lux was excited it was on a night Leslie Odom, Jr performed. He was so excited he spent most of our dinner talking about the show and Odom's music that I actually started getting annoyed.

In times past, I'd mentioned how much I liked the late singer Aaliyah. He wasn't familiar with her work. Likely because her music was stalled on distribution, for reasons I didn't understand and because he normally listens to only jazz or instrumental music.

Knowing how much he likes dancing, I told him I wanted to show him some old videos of her dancing. But I had other plans. When we got back to our suite, I did pull up her song, *More Than a*

*Woman,* on YouTube, but I only let it play while I started moving playfully to the beat.

Sitting on the bed, Lux was merely entertained at first. Then I started undressing while I was dancing. Wearing my fishnet hose underneath my little black cocktail dress, I'm sure he wasn't prepared to learn I wasn't wearing panties.

Adorned in nothing but my hosiery, a black laced bra, and high heels, I knew my dance was getting to him as I saw the tent lift beneath his slacks. Taking in heavy breaths as his eyes followed my every move, Lux Decanter was completely under my spell.

Before I knew it, Lux ripped my bra off, taking both of my breasts in his hands, sucking on them like a thirsty man. Bursting through his own outfit in mid-shift, nothing but his boxers remained as I finally got to behold my beloved almost bare before me.

Lux had always been so careful. Perhaps it was because we were always in Nova Scotia, he felt respect for my parents. But this was one of our first times traveling alone. He had always found a way to drag Cedric and Abigail along, like chaperones. He insisted that since his presence around them helps quench their bloodlust, they owed him a favor.

Thankfully, us girls stick together. Somehow Cedric and Abigail missed their flight to New

## Chapter Thirty-Two

York. To this day Abigail insists she thought the flight was for a later date. Although Cedric didn't buy it, he went along with it, because he hates theatre.

While I hoped this would finally be our moment, Lux had more willpower than I imagined. Yet not *that* much.

*"Why are you tempting me like this?" Lux insisted as his hands explored my body.*

*"Because I need this, baby,"* I moaned, pulling him so close I could feel the bulge beneath his boxers. *"It hurts baby, I need you,"* I cried. Those weren't crocodile tears. My sweet spot was aching for him. *"I—I tried but I couldn't,"* I shamefully admitted to my failed attempts at curing my own arousal.

"That's because it's only for me to do," Lux said, running his hands along my sex. Panting, he whispered, "You want to come, don't you sweetness?" Nodding only, I mouthed yes, but the words couldn't come out. "Okay, this one time, but that's all. And you'll have to do it my way."

"Anything, please, Lux," I begged.

*"The heels and the stockings stay on!" He ordered, flashing his golden eyes. Nodding once more, he dropped his face to my sex, inhaling me wholly. "You smell so sweet, baby. Let me see how you taste." Ripping the hose at the seam of my crotch, Lux's tongue plunged inside me. Cir-*

cling his tongue and nipping at the sensitive skin of my sex, he expertly willed me into a frenzy. Awakening my passionate pixie to heights we could only imagine, I clawed at the sheets at my sides trying to contain my screams.

After sampling me, Lux lifted himself, looking sexy as ever as he wiped my arousal from his goatee.

"You're even sweeter than I hoped," Lux said. "Now your little song said, I wasn't ready, but it's you who needs to be ready. Tempting me like this. I can't stay down there too long or I'm going in, and when I do, I'm not coming out. But I can't risk it without making you my wife."

"We can try, baby, I can take it. I promise. At least let me try," Reaching out, my hands gripped his manhood, beneath his boxers. Massaging up and down, he grunted, as I needed both of my hands to accommodate his erection. His skin was smooth and perfect, just as I imagined. "At least let me return the favor, I said, inviting him into my mouth.

"Oh no you don't, Winter," he said, painfully pulling away. "I told you, my rules. Now let me help relieve your pain." With two fingers on my sweet spot, he tapped my entrance. "So since you're nice and wet, I can help you. Just relax, baby. Let me explore you."

## Chapter Thirty-Two

*"Please," I moaned back. And explored me he did. Twirling, thrusting, and tapping, his fingers found the spot. "That's it, baby!" I cried out.*

*"Your first one was supposed to be on your throne, but I think I need this too." Lux's strained tone was hard to miss but when he grabbed my hand and placed it around his girth, I knew exactly what he needed. "Oh baby, we're doing this together," he directed, groaning with each tug on my sex. "Now, baby now!" he roared.*

*My first orgasm sent jolts of electricity through my body I never knew existed until that moment. But I wasn't prepared for Lux to do what he did next. Just as my climax reached its peak, he quickly shoved his tongue back into my spot, lapping everything I had to give, sending me into another frenzy. Fearful my screams would alert those in the hotel, I plunged my fist into my mouth. Covered with all Lux had to give in return, I licked my hand clean, relishing every drop.*

*Looking up at me, through darkened eyes, and once more covered with my arousal, a sexy smirk danced at the corner of Lux's mouth as he watched me take in the last morsel.*

*We fell asleep in each other's arms, but when I felt Lux's member tapping my backside, I thought for sure we were headed for the next round. But Lux's restraint kicked back in. A little.*

*"Don't worry baby, the next time I see you, I'm taking everything that's mine,"* he said plunging his fingers back inside, making me whimper.

Lux left that night. He caught the red eye back to Louisiana and stayed there until today, citing he couldn't trust what I'd do next.

Recalling the sweet memories of our last encounter, my heart races knowing I'll finally marry the man I love. Now here I am, standing in front of my mirror all dressed in white, wondering indeed, when I see my husband tonight under a moonlit sky, what will I do next.

A knock at the door forces me from my ruminations. The door cracks, and my father's smiling face peeks in. I faintly hear Odom's *Heaven & Earth* playing from afar as my dad asks, "Ready to become Mrs. Decanter?"

"Yes, Father," I smile back, staring into his glassy eyes. I am more than ready.

# Chapter Thirty-Three

*Lux*

I thought our wedding was beautiful. So beautiful in fact, my eyes ran like a river from the moment Lord Elysian escorted my lovely bride down the aisle until the final moments we both said, *I do*.

But seeing Winter bare beneath me now, her legs outstretched, ready to receive me as her husband is the most beautiful delight my eyes have ever witnessed.

There is only one thing I need before we begin. "I just need you to say it, baby. Tell me who you are," my words are desperate as she grinds beneath me, pushing her sex up, teasing me. Her arousal hits my nose, stiffening my manhood harder than I've ever been. Although I scented and tasted her back in New York, her pheromones are peaking more than before.

She must be ovulating.

If she is, my wolf will be insatiable, and this night may never end.

Although Winter has seen me shift before, seeing my wolf during intimacy is a different matter altogether. My wolf will speak to her in ways the language of men is too confined to allow.

"I am yours. Your wife," she whispers back, lightly dragging her fingers through my hair.

"Yes, you are Mrs. Decanter. *All mine!*" I growl and my wolf is released.

The flash of gold is brighter than usual as I see it reflected in her eyes as my wolf connects with her.

*Do you feel that Winter? Want it?* My wolf roars within me.

"Oh, Lux!" Winter whines beneath me. "Yes, I want it, please!" Her reply tells me she is speaking directly to my wolf. Which can only mean he has fully accepted her.

*Thank the Moon!*

Pushing her hips up, her sex aligns with my tip and within seconds I ease inside her. She's snug as she winces a bit, moving her hips trying to get comfortable. I've heard women say their mates

## Chapter Thirty-Three

are bigger than normal during ritual mating. I'm not sure if that's true. I'll let my wife be the judge.

"Are you okay, baby?" I ask, brushing my hand through her hair. I want to take my time with her. I don't want to hurt her. Not ever.

*Set me free. I hear my wolf say.*

"Yes baby," she coos, looking up at me through trusting eyes. "But I want it to hurt, Lux. I want to feel everything. Please!"

Neither Winter nor my wolf are going to let me off easy tonight.

"Happy to oblige," I answer, shoving the rest of myself into my wife. Her nails dig into my shoulders as she cries out in both pleasure and pain. But like all things it doesn't take my baby long to learn something new. Once she adjusts to my size, it's not just me, but Winter thrusting her hips upward, demanding everything I have to give. If I'm not careful, my wolf and Winter will have me releasing all I have before I'm ready.

Locking our lips together, our kiss is more fervent than ever. Desperate. In no time, Winter is straddled at my waist, breasts bouncing in my face, screaming my name. She is driving me crazy. I thought this would be the moment I'd fill her with all of me, but my new bride is just as insatiable, if not more so than my wolf.

That's how I know our mating ritual is working.

Pushing me down with her newly inherited strength, my wife bucks, and grinds on top of me as though my manhood was her personal healing balm.

Reaching on the nightstand, Winter grabs her crown. A sly smile crosses her face when she hands it to me as she continues grinding on top of me. "Put it on me," she orders, lowering her head and leaning over so that her perky breasts are once more in my face.

But her change of position, instantly shifts the control back to me. With one hand on her hips and the other placing the crown on her head, I thrust my hips upward, hitting her spot, causing her sweetness to run down her legs, soaking me. She tries to pull up, but I keep her in this position with a tightened hold at her back.

"Come on baby, enjoy your throne," I smirk, watching her face contort as she sits on the edge of her orgasm.

"Lux, please," she begs. "It's coming, baby!" Riding me harder, my wife explodes in tidal waves of passion. My newly crowned queen vibrates against me, sending my wolf into relentless overdrive.

Collapsing onto my chest, Winter is breathless as she continues to pulsate around me. But my wolf is far from finished. Flipping us over, my erection hardens more than I thought myself capable and my wolf howls through me as I pound into my wife, discovering her depths as her sweet nectar soaks the sheets.

## Chapter Thirty-Three

And Winter is taking all I have to give. Just when I thought she's had enough, her eyes brighten as I plunge into her once more, awakening the vixen who now wears the crown. Meeting my thrusts, my wife trails her hands along my chest and biceps, each touch sending new vigor to my manhood, making me feel worthy of everything she's giving me.

A loud roar rumbles through me, shaking the room as our headboard bangs hard against the wall. "I'm giving you all of me Mrs. Decanter!" Growling my words, my ecstasy explodes into her depths, filling her with more than I thought possible.

But my wolf isn't done.

He still needs to imprint.

Now that the essence of my wolf has entered her body, I need to mark her.

Winter's eyes widen when she notices my hardened member.

"Baby, I don't know if I can take any more," Winter says, keeping her eyes locked on my girth.

"I know you can, Winter," I say, stroking her sweet spot, feeling the wetness of both of us there. Whimpering as my hand taps her entrance once more, she wiggles beneath me, reviving her interest.

"Oh maybe once more," she says grabbing my length. "But damn, baby did it get bigger?" Her eyes look back at me with shock. "Lux, I don't think that monster will fit."

"Just trust me," I say, swirling my finger in her depths. She cries out, stimulated by my touch and my wolf responds with a roar. "I need to imprint on you. Do you trust me, Winter?"

"Yes, Lux," she moans, grinding against my palm. Sliding my fingers out, I lean over her and work myself inside her once more. She flinches a bit as my now enlarged size primes her opening and she cries out in pleasure. "More!"

Little does she know; this part will be new for both of us. I've never mated or imprinted before. I'm just following the lead of my wolf. Pressing myself deep inside her, we both groan as the pleasure overwhelms us as nothing but growls rumble through me. How my wife's small frame can contain the width of me, I'll never know, but I thank her for trusting me.

Nuzzling our noses once more, my pace slows as I take her hand in mine, allowing myself to be lost in her eyes. The love we share is incomparable.

Howling as the moon reaches its apex, my muscles constrict as if I were to shift, but instead the weight of me presses into Winter, releasing the totality of my essence upon her, imprinting on her completely. Her body shimmers with a radiant glow beneath me and her eyes, too, flash, mirroring the glow of my own. Although I've seen wolfen eyes all my life, seeing them in my wife sends me into a frenzy.

In fact, it's the sexiest thing ever!

*Winter is my wife. I love her. My wolf resounds within me.*

Just as I said at the altar, I love her with my whole life, mind, body, and soul. Her life is now my life. Her body mine as mine is now hers. Between us there is only co-mission. My devotion to her is just as submissive as I'll ever ask of her. She is my equal. My mate. I am her protector. Her guardian. I protect what I love because I love to protect. And I protect what is mine.

"This is mine, Winter!" I say, picking up my pace, pounding harder.

"All yours," she grinds against me. "Take it, my king, take it!" she shouts as we reach our peak together.

And take it I shall, from this day forward.

# Chapter Thirty-Four

## *Winter*

Lux didn't really give me an opportunity to truly appreciate my wedding gift. Carrying me straight over the threshold to our bedroom, it was clear with the constant wolfen glow in his eyes, my newly pronounced husband had one thing on his mind. Now, with the mid-morning light of the sun, I finally have a chance to walk about the redesigned cabin that is now our home.

The place where we shared our first kiss.

Knowing both Lux and my father worked on this together makes me even happier. When Lux first came into my life, I never thought the two would ever see eye to eye. I've never been so glad to be wrong. In fact, as Lux has told me, the time he spent with my father redesigning the house helped him understand my father in a whole new light; and vice versa.

During their time together Lux talked in length about his upbringing. He shared how he met my great-great grandmother Greta. While he only knew her for a short time when he first moved to Louisiana, he described her as a kind and generous woman. Lux even said how she worked to free slaves and provide food for their journey. I think learning more about our heritage from Lux helped my father connect with him on a deeper level.

While I wanted Lux to show me everything he's done in the cabin himself, he insisted I take my time touring it on my own while he worked on breakfast. I suppose it's the least he could do after ravaging my body the way he did last night.

And considering the fact he continued pounding into me well into this morning, it's a wonder I can walk.

My husband did spend a considerable time showing me around the ginormous spa retreat he calls an en suite. With a large steam shower, including dual showerheads for two and a large soaking tub, Lux was more than delighted to help acquaint me with our new home via a demonstration of sorts.

## Chapter Thirty-Four

After starting the dewy mist setting of our shower, Lux insisted we rinse off our residue from our mating before we indulged in a warm, milky rose petal bath. Not that it wasn't enough my husband woke me up with a spooning to my rear this morning, but when he bent me over the shower bench, I knew the primal wolf within him was indeed awake.

Not stopping at taking me from behind but delighting himself with a luscious lap at my sex that had my arousal leaking down his chin, he finally gave in and let me return the favor. Even now, memories of me seated on the bench with the glory of him filling my mouth as the dew covered our bodies, reinvigorates parts of me I've only just begun to discover.

But I wasn't prepared for my husband to make sweet love to me in our bath. Once we left the shower, I was sure we'd only soak and bathe. Yet another time I'm thankful to be wrong. Seating me on top of him, Lux rocked us to heights of ecstasy I was sure only existed in fantasy. I never knew I was capable of the mewling sounds coming from me as he held me in his arms, thrusting into me over and over.

Every ounce of energy I had left me once I reached my climax. Carrying me back to our bed, Lux laid me down, sweetly kissing me. Although I know a part of Lux wanted to let me rest, I heard his wolf call to me, begging me for more. A bashful, yet knowing glance hovered over Lux's face as he looked at me and I reached down only to discover his stiffened manhood. Grabbing his rear, I pulled him close, and my husband was more than happy to resume his duties.

Thankfully, Lux was gentle with me. Slowly rotating his hips, his rhythmic motion lulled me into a state of bliss so sweet, I fell asleep after melting all over him. I so hope this isn't only part of the mating ritual. I could certainly get used to enjoying this.

Again, how I'm capable of walking around our home now is beyond me.

I'm impressed by Lux's designs. He's pretty good with wood. *Go figure.*

The extra rooms, Jack and Jill bathroom, and office he added look like they've been here all along. There's both a rustic charm with a mid-century feel, complementing our individual styles.

Lux has taken care to leave little notes and trinkets for me in almost every space of the house, denoting his intent. Most notably are the two rooms with teddy bears wearing respective pink and blue ribbons, placed in the window seal of each room. I can't help but thinking he's already knocked me up, with the way we've gone at it. Laughing, I chuckle thinking how he'll probably

## Chapter Thirty-Four

want to name our son Odom and daughter Leslie. I'll certainly coax him off that path if need be.

More surprising is the bonus loft he added. It's a craft room for me. Although all roads are leading to the opening of Regency Academy, my husband has paid special attention to my love for crafting and design. When he discovered I put together all of the ornaments for last year's cotillion, he began encouraging me to sell a few pieces online. While my sales have been modest, even I am surprised at how well my little side business is doing.

The fact that Lux believes in me means everything. This room is proof.

Picking up a small notecard, tears well in my eyes as I read my husband's words.

*"To my wife,*

*Our love is proof dreams do come true. My one goal in life is to encourage and inspire you to pursue your every dream and desire. From schools to crafts. From children to family. For everything in between. Keep on dreaming, baby. I'll be right here when you awake.*

*Dream Well,*

*Your Husband."*

"And I meant every word," Lux's deep voice calls to me from behind, startling me from a joyfully weepy moment. Standing at the top of the stairs, my husband is now fully dressed in joggers and a tee. Thank the Moon! I don't think I could handle another round.

Walking toward me, Lux lays a folded piece of clothing on the craft table. Falling into his arms, loose tears of joy fall to my cheeks as he squeezes me tight.

"This is all so lovely, baby," I mutter, trying to compose myself. "How did you even have time to do this? Between your work with the Guard and travels from here to Louisiana. And all the work you've put in with helping me get the school started—"

"Winter, I'd add ten more hours to my day to ensure your happiness. Because your happiness is my happiness. How many times do I have to tell you that?" He laughs, nuzzling our noses as his wolf croons through his chest, settling my angst.

Kissing my lips softly, Lux presses his forehead to mine and breathes me in. He likes doing that.

"Every chance you get," I whisper into the cavity of his hold.

"I think I can handle that." Squeezing me tighter, I take a moment to inhale my husband. He smells of crisp linen and bacon. My stomach growls against him and he chuckles. "Well, sounds like my wife has a hungry wolf inside her all her own—or could that be a new little Decanter already?" He adds, leaning down to my stomach.

## Chapter Thirty-Four

Playfully shoving his shoulder, I shake my head at my husband's eagerness to get me pregnant so soon. "I'm just hungry Mr. Decanter!" I laugh as he holds his head against my abdomen.

"Well, I'm glad," he smirks, tossing me a pair of yoga pants and a bra. "Because breakfast is ready. Now put these on because we have company." Still smiling, Lux's eyes flit over my shoulder downstairs.

"Yeah, and we're getting hungry!" I hear Ross yell up the stairs.

Confused, I snatch the pants from Lux, working them up as he wrangles my shirt to help me with my bra.

"Lux?"

Only gesturing his hand for me to head downstairs, we make our way down. I am surprised to find my family in the area where Lux once healed Ross. The room is now a dining area with a table large enough to seat twelve.

Seeing my parents, Melchior, Ross, Rae, Stephen, Cedric and Abigail all seated at the table warms my heart. Once more, I feel my eyes well with tears at the smiles greeting both Lux and me. Even Rae seems happier than she's been in the last year. Just seeing a return of my cousin's more chipper self is enough to make me leap for joy.

"Everyone, thanks for joining us this morning," Lux starts with a small kiss to my forehead. "It is customary after the mating ritual for the pack—or family in this instance—our pack to commemorate with a meal. In this, we mark our connection as family. Always and forever."

With another kiss, Lux seats us at the head of our table and I look around, thankful for everyone here. This is all I ever wanted.

# Epilogue

## *Winter*

*Three Years Later*

"I can't believe we're graduating!" Cassidy squeals, twirling around the stage of the auditorium. "I mean, like, this is really happening!" She jumps, practicing throwing her cap off her head.

Theadra looks over her shoulder, allowing a small smile, but her eyes roll and I know she's grown tired of her best friend, Cassidy, and her constant interruptions. Although she's too sweet to say it.

"Cassidy, I know you're excited, but Theadra wants to finish practicing her valedictorian speech. You're making her nervous," I say, rubbing my round belly. My babies are extremely active today. Either they're just as excited as Cassidy about graduation or they are little Olympians in the making.

"I'm fine, Mrs. Decanter," Theadra laughs, darting her eyes to her boyfriend Travis as he shapes his hands into a heart at his chest while looking up at her from the front row.

"Aren't they adorable," I whisper over my shoulder as I feel my husband's strong arms wrap around my waist from behind. I could hear his wolf call to me before he got this close.

Lux rubs my belly, kissing my neck as he inhales deeply, breathing me in. "Perhaps, but no one looks more adorable than my beautiful pregnant wife."

Laughing over my shoulder, I give him a quick peck on the lips, but I turn my attention back to the stage. My mind sifts over every detail of tomorrow's graduation. I hope I haven't forgotten anything.

"Stop trying to distract me, Lux," I chuckle, attempting to wiggle out of his hold. But my husband keeps his grip firm, ensuring I feel the hardnening of him at my bottom. Letting out a small gasp, I shake my head, my husband knows how insatiable I've become the closer I get to my due date.

I gave birth to our first son only six months

*Epilogue*

after our wedding. We named him Cedric after Lux's brother but we call him Ric. Being as though my in laws can never have their own children, Lux and I thought it only fitting. Since wolf children have a shorter gestation than humans, I never thought I'd be able to get the school off the ground while tending to my newfound role as a mom. Especially so soon. However, my pack is the best. Abigail loves on Little Ric as if he were her own while my mother has found a whole new joy in life in being a Nana.

Thanks to all of the support we've garnered, we were still able to get the school started right away.

It couldn't have come at a better time.

After the world took a spin on its axis when the events from Dalcour's relationship with Damina took a nose dive and her cousin, Dacari, unknowingly unleashed a new dark threat into the world, supernatural children needed a place to call their own, now more than ever.

Just as Lux suggested.

And with Regency Academy welcoming both mortal and supernatural young regents, we have students as young as five and as old as eighteen, like Cassidy, Theadra, and Travis; our first students.

Thankfully, however, the chaos once threatening to implode our world from the havoc brought on by Dalcour, Damina, and Dacari has ended. As much as I hate to admit it, we have Kharon to thank for that. His understanding of the Netherworld and Changelings, aided Lord Nashoba in defeating the darkness once and for all. For that, I'm finally learning to make peace with Rae and Kharon's relationship.

Still as I lean back into Lux's embrace, I can't help the lone tear that falls to my cheek when I think of all it took to see this day come to pass.

When Trieu brought our first supernatural students, Travis and Theadra, to the school three years ago, I really didn't know how this would all work out. Even though they arrived under duress, both Travis and Theadra welcomed the opportunity to learn more about their newfound supernaturality from their teachers like my brother-in-law Cedric, Kharon, and Trieu. We've even had Dalcour and Damina as guest lecturers from time to time.

Lux, on the other hand, chooses to keep his focus on the Guard. Training new regents and ensuring no new threats make their way onto the island. Although we haven't had a breach in years, he insists he will not risk the safety of our family or any under his care.

"I'm proud of you," Lux breathes into my ear, distracting me from my musing.

Wiping my face, I turn to find his super sexy smile, grinning back at me. "For what?" I ask, wiping my face with my wrist.

*Epilogue*

"For all of this," he answers, extending his hand around the auditorium. I smile as I watch Travis take Theadra's notebooks in his hand and he aids her down the stairs. Cassidy follows them, shouting in glee as they travel down the hall where other students are removing decorations from last night's prom. "You did this, baby and I am so proud of you." Lux's golden eyes flash at me as he speaks and the admiration I see in his smile makes my heart melt.

Running my hand through his wavy tendrils, I am in awe at strapping stallion staring back at me. I love him so much. "*We* did this. I could have never done any of it without you."

Kissing my forehead, Lux seals his lips against the crown of my head, while holding me firm at my back. "And you'll never have to, baby. That is a promise I'll always keep."

Breathing in his words, the thought of my love for Lux shoots straight to my sweet spot. I glance up at the clock on the wall and notice we have another hour before we need to pick Ric up from my parents and inspiration strikes.

"Well, then since we're making promises, why don't you take me home. I want to give you what I promised would always be yours. That is, if you're up to it."

Pushing himself against me, I feel his stiffness jutting against my abdomen. "Yep, I'm up for it. Let's go home."

*And we lived happily ever after.*

**The End.**

# Order of Altrinion
## Regent Hierarchy

**Changeling**
First born of Non-Earth Supernaturals. Powers of darkness, wind, and shadow. Cursed to a formless void after rebellion of the Order.
Death only by a blade dipped in the Sacred Waters.

**Changeling jinn**
Bound by Keepers of the Order to golden jars of clay; destined to oblige the masters of their keep
May only reclaim form through sacrificial procreation of earthbound souls; mortal and supernatural alike

**Harbingers & praesidiums**
Remnants of the world long past. Bulwarks, Gargoyles, Dragons, Deities and Gorgons.
Relegated to both Earthbound and the dark world. Watchkeepers & Gatekeepers.

**Wolves**
Earthbound lycan kin. Grand protectors of the Order.

**Prime & Omega Wolves**
Non tertiary of lunar ascendency. Primes hold purview of Dunes, Pack, and all other wolfen-kind. Not subject to lunar cycle; may change at will. Omega hold purview of all. Titlular ascendents
 Pack & Dunes Wolves- bound to the manner of lunar succession;

**Prime & Omega Wolves**
Non tertiary of lunar ascendency. Primes hold purview of Dunes, Pack, and all other wolfen-kind. Not subject to lunar

cycle; may change at will. Omega hold purview of all. Titlular ascendents
Pack & Dunes Wolves- bound to the manner of lunar succession;

## Altrinion
First born of Earthborn Supernaturals. Strength of the wind, earth, sky and strengthened by the sun. Ability to read mortal minds.
Death only by obsidian blade or self-sacrifice through the Sacred Waters.

## Altrinion-Vampires
Cursed by the blood of mortals once a mortal life is taken and forever destined to crave the humans they were bound to watchover.
Cursed never to walk in the light of the sun; unless by selfless love they redeem their soul. Progenitor of all mortal-made vampires
Death by Obsidian blade or the Sun

## Scourge Vampires
Mortal made; not of the Order of Altrinion
Cursed by blood; savage and bloodthirsty. Commands power of the sky.
Death by the Sun, decapitation, or mortal wound

## The Curse of Skull Wolves
By the order of Altrinion, all earthbound will abide by the form of man. Walking this earth in his likeness and stature, wolves of lunar succession must not be found deserted, barren, or lacking earthbound affinity or mammon.
Dereliction is akin to apostasy. Wolves forgone as such break the bonds of succession and kinship of MAN; forever cursed to a hollowed, soulless form. A skull. A desolate monstrosity.

# Want More?

Get a FREE bonus short story of Rae & Kharon's darkly enchanting romance.

## *Fire Kissed*

Hold your sails, this hot story is steamboat!

Go here to claim your FREE bonus story now.

[My Books & Short Stories - L. C. Son Books (lcsonbooks.com)](https://lcsonbooks.com)

*Available for a limited time only*

# More from L.C. Son…

Here are a few more books and short stories in the Beautiful Nightmare Universe:

## **Books**

Beautiful Nightmare (Book One)

Hearts Eclipsed, A Beautiful Nightmare Novella

Awaken: Beautiful Nightmare (Book Two)

Untamed: A Beautiful Nightmare Story

Breaking Curses: A Beautiful Nightmare Novella- Planned 2022

Beta Rising: A Beautiful Nightmare Novella- Coming Soon!

Beautifully Dark Things- Planned 2023

Dawn of Descent: Beautiful Nightmare (Book Three) TBA

## **Short Stories**

I AM NO WITCH: A Beautiful Nightmare Short Story

With Clipped Wings of Butterflies: A Beautiful Nightmare Short Story

With Hearts Like Fire: A Beautiful Nightmare Short Story

**For more info on my books, visit:**

[My Books & Short Stories - L. C. Son Books (lcsonbooks.com)](lcsonbooks.com)

Remember leaving reviews makes you a MVP!!

Thank you!

# About L.C. Son

Known for her Amazon Best Selling Short Story, **With Hearts Like Fire** and the series starter and epic fantasy novel, **Beautiful Nightmare (Book One)**, L.C. Son is the happy wife of more than twenty years to her teenage sweetheart and the loving mom of three.

Growing up, she spent hours reading comic books she "borrowed" from her older brother which inspired her love for heroes and all things fantasy and paranormal. Much like the characters she adored, she lives a duplicitous life. By day she works tirelessly to champion the employment of persons with severe disabilities. By night, she puts on her wife-mom cape, sharing with her husband at their church and juggling their kid's highly active schedules.

Presently, she's working on the next installment in the Beautiful Nightmare series.

For the latest info and to join the member-only newsletter visit:

www.lcsonbooks.com